Fragments I Saved from the Fire

Fragments I Saved from the Fire

Stories by Mary Anne Ashley

Papier-Mache Press
Watsonville, California

Copyright © 1989 by Papier-Mache Press. All rights reserved including the right to reproduce this book or portions thereof in any form. For information contact Papier-Mache Press, 795 Via Manzana, Watsonville, California, 95076-9154, (408) 726-2933.

First Edition

Printed in the United States of America.

93 92 91 90 89   6 5 4 3 2 1

Copyediting: Jo Ann Meredith.
Design: Cynthia Heier.
Cover art: Valera Crystle, acrylic portrait, "Sylvia"
Valera Crystle is a resident of Sonoma, California. She has studied at the Academy of Art in San Francisco and is currently writing and illustrating children's books.

Grateful acknowledgement is made to the following publications which first published some of the material in this book: *Quindaro 14* and *Quindaro 15* (Edited by Fred Whitehead, 1984), *Midwest Villages & Voices* (Spring 1987), and *When I Am an Old Woman I Shall Wear Purple* (Papier-Mache Press, 1987).

Library of Congress Cataloging in Publication Data.

Ashley, Mary Anne, 1934-
  Fragments I saved from the fire: stories/by Mary Anne Ashley. — 1st ed.
    p. cm.
  ISBN: 0-918949-06-8 : $9.00
  1. California—Fiction. I. Title.
PS3551.S3786F7 1989   89-16251
813'.54—dc20   CIP

My thanks go to JoAnne, Lisa, Carroll, Sylvia, Jim, and Meridel. Special thanks go to Don Meredith.

Contents

Deja Vu
- 3   What Is This? Deja Vu?
- 19   The Delta in Between
- 21   Early Days in Acampo

The Salinas Streak
- 27   Meet the Salinas Streak
- 29   There Is Something about BoBo
- 31   Love Drives
- 37   Heart Wattle
- 41   BoBo's Christmas BooBoo

Good Elements
- 47   Good Elements
- 53   Justice for Consuelo
- 57   Consuelo Loves Night Tire
- 59   It's the American Way
- 65   The Beach

DEAR JOANNE

71 Dear JoAnne
79 Juke Box Dancer
81 You Could Have Named Her Grande
83 The Woman Who Likes to Fall Down
85 Airstream

GRACEFULLY AFRAID

89 Gracefully Afraid
101 The Tiger Lily

EPILOGUE

105 Red Stone, Blue Stone

Deja Vu

During sultry, dry weather, and often preceding a thunderstorm, Nasturtiums, Marigolds, and Oriental Poppies throw small flashes of light.

Garden Gimmicks
Marceline, Missouri, 1953

What Is This? Deja Vu?

More and more these days I find myself thinking about Sacramento, California. Sacramento in the thirties. And me and Margaret O'Shea. Margaret was my best friend. I loved her. A lot of people did. Only lately have I understood why. She was such a mess. But such a lovely, laffing mess. And she suggested possibilities that were beyond our ordinary dreams. Possibilities about herself, possibilities about us.

I'm going to be famous one day, she'd say. Her eyes looked off and way up high. One day I'll be a great person.

Yeah, I said. Great. Doing what?

I don't know yet. It doesn't matter. You're going to be great, too. We're special people. That's why other people don't understand us, think we're odd. We are odd. Great people are always odd.

Gawd, Margaret, you kill me.

When I first met Margaret in 1931, she lived in a rented room on H Street, 1226 H Street. She came to Sacto from Houston, or Washington, or Kansas City, depending on which story she told that day. She'd just been married. That part was true. I saw the certificate. She married Neil (short for Cornelius) O'Shea down in New Mexico in January. By March she was living alone.

No job, no money, looking for work, and wondering where her next meal would come from. Neil and his brother Mike had left. Just dumped her. I never could stand Neil or Mike.

When Margaret filed for divorce in 1936, it was largely due to my good persuasion. A pretty bold thing to do in '36, especially when you consider she was Catholic. So were Neil and Mike. So was I. Almost everybody I knew in those days was either Catholic or Communist, or both. Lots of people ran around with Communists. Not like later when you swore you never even knew what the word meant. The Commies were the only ones who seemed to know what was going on—the Commies and the Anarchists. They knew why we were out of work, why we were so poor, why we were so down. They were the only ones who had a plan.

I always thought the Commies were like Wobblies, but when I said that to Dad, he yelled, If you ever say that again, I'll throw you out on your ear, which was pretty funny since I hadn't been living at home since the 11th grade.

During the Great Strike of 1919, Dad had been in Seattle with the IWW when they took over the city for three days and tried to get it unionized. Later, Dad was still union, but pretty conservative. Those days, he said, were all behind him. Leave it to the younger boys, he said. One night Dad slapped me and called me a dammed radical. That's the kind of Wobblie he became.

That's the night I left home. Moved out, bag and baggage. Walked out and slammed the door. Quit school. I never looked back, as the old saying goes, and even with some of the hard times I've known since, I never regretted it. Not once.

Truth is, I'd been running around with the Reds ever since I heard Nora Conklin give a speech in City Park Plaza. She stood up tall, talked to the crowd, and shook her fist. She made more sense than any woman I'd ever heard. She knew more than any woman I'd ever met. I felt in my heart that I was the true, long lost daughter of Nora Conklin, fighter for the poor, fighter for the working class, fighter for the oppressed. And if that wasn't the real story, it was awfully close to it.

So, no wonder then that I took Margaret O'Shea up to meet Nora for some straight talk and help in those terrible Great Depression days. (Years later, Margaret and I sat together during Nora's trial, and wept when the verdict was read.) Nora ran the Unemployed Council from a little office on 12th Street. We went there a lot to read the papers, have a cup of coffee, get in out of the rain, sit somewhere friendly during the long, grey days of searching for work. We searched like treasure seekers, but instead of looking in ferns and down wells, behind trees and under rocks, we looked in dim places with grimy windows; we peered through plate glass into rooms where folks looked well fed; we looked down alleys, into doorways; and one day we stood staring down into the gutter, thinking: Where do we go now? What do we do next? Some days we would be so down, so hopeless that we'd just stare at one another, the way the newly dead must stare at the newly dead. Sometimes we just fell into chairs and checked our stockings for runs and said, Honest-to-gawd. Can it get worse? Can it be this bad?

But we knew it was this bad, all right. Like when sweet, chubby Mildred, fresh from a farm in Lodi, sweet and round as one of the watermelons her family grew, unemployed Mildred, evicted Mildred, gave herself an abortion in the ladies' restroom at the Bon Ton Department Store. Aborted herself right out of this world. So long, Mildred, and fare-thee-well. You bet things were this bad. Like when we found out about Hazel. Funny old Hazel. Tap-dancing, spaghetti-eating Hazel. Finger-snapping, eyes-flashing Hazel, so in love with finger-snapping, eyes-flashing Tom. Who was really her pimp.

Yes, Hazel had been selling her body to stay alive in a nasty little room in one of those nasty little hotels on Jay Street. And we would have never known if her folks hadn't come to town from down in Santa Barbara, called in the cops and raised a stink that was in all the papers for weeks. They took Hazel home and put her in an insane asylum. Well, so long, Hazel, and fare-thee-well.

Yes, you bet it was this bad, so bad that those same things could have happened to Margaret and me. But they didn't. Very bad things happened, but not quite that bad. Somehow Margaret and I stayed halfway between Hazel and Mildred (crazy and dead) and Doris and Verleen (happy and making it).

Doris ran a dance studio on 35th Street in Oak Park, and later on Jay Street, upstairs, 1019 Jay Street. I used to call her "The Tap Dancing Socialist," and she'd say, Don't call me that. Why do you call me that? And I'd say, Why do I call you that? Because you know every Bolshevik who ever came to town and always live right next door to six. You're the only one ready to rent meeting-room space to the Workers Alliance. Doris, what a card, but she wasn't out of work. She knew how to get along, usually on her own. And she knew how to make room for others.

Margaret and Hazel used to hang around a lot in Doris's studio on Jay. They went up there and tap danced all afternoon, laffing and tapping, and shaking the blues away, just like in the Ruth Etting song. Doris never liked Margaret as much as she liked Hazel, Verleen, and me. She said that Margaret was whiny and weak-spined. Well, maybe she was sometimes. You would be too if you had two kids farmed out with a wild woman in Folsom, no job, no money, no family to love you. But if she was sometimes snivelly, she more often was not. She was tough inside. Soft on the outside but tough on the inside. Verleen and Doris just naturally gravitated toward each other because they were the only ones who worked steady.

Verleen first had a job as a playground attendant, then took a test and got a job clerking with the City Parks and Recreation. She was the one who found Margaret her WPA job, working as a playground attendant. Just like Verleen used to. It seemed a good omen. But it wasn't.

Verleen loved to take Margaret home to have dinner with her family because Margaret always looked like a lady. She was neat as a pin, and pretty in a quiet sort of way. The kind who always shook her clothes out when she took them off, hand washed her undies, mended her stockings and gloves with tiny neat stitches, brushed her hair one hundred strokes before bedtime, went without lunch for a week to have her shoes reheeled and resoled. She was the kind who sat with her feet crossed at the ankles, knew exactly when to say "please" and "thank you." These were the things Nora and I tried to change. But Verleen's folks thought it was marvelous that their daughter palled around with such a "good element." It relieved their minds because Verleen was downtown so much. At night, too. We were all hanging around the dance halls, that's what we were doing.

sobbing in a vacant room.
screaming in a long, dark tunnel
a gun going off in the library.

That's what Margaret had written on a piece of paper I found lying on her dresser one night.
What's this, I asked.
That's me, she said.

So, what's *that* supposed to mean?

I wanted to smart off and act wise, but what she wrote made me nervous. What she wrote sounded like her. I liked what she wrote, but it scared me. So I flicked an imaginary hair off my shoulder and said, "A gun going off in the library." Honest-to-gawd, Margaret, you're a laff riot. You really are.

That was the night she met Van. I should have known something terrible was going to happen.

We used to hang around a lot at the Buffalo Club on 19th and S Streets. One reason was because Margaret had a room upstairs for a while, where we could run up to see her. Another was that from time to time the fellows that we ran around with had jobs at the Buffalo Brewery around the corner, and we'd meet them for a drink when they finished their shifts. But the main reason was because the Buffalo Club was a great place to dance. It had smooth dance floors, big booths, and a juke box, one of the best. Did we love to dance! Sometimes we danced all night and worked all day, if we were lucky, then danced again all night. We were dancing fools.

Well, we were dancing up a storm one night with Homer and Sis Maier, Doris and Hazel, Tom and Verleen, and some lefties from Berkeley, when in walks this sharp dresser, short guy, real particular, real precise. I knew I didn't like him the minute I saw him. One of those heavy drinkers, a seen-better-times kind of guy, a wise-acre, but something else under there. You know the kind I mean? Elmer Vanderhoofven to give him his full name. Not Hoff, he'd say. Hoof! Hoof! That's not too hard to remember now, is it?

What a snot of a guy he was. I thought that then, and I thought it in 1965 when he dropped dead in William

Land Park. Just the kind of guy Margaret didn't need. And just the kind of guy she always went gaga over. Just like Neil. And, if you ask me, probably just like her dad. Yes, she liked him, and their disastrous affair lasted, off and on, over five years. A lot of people liked him, but never me. To give him his due, Van was terribly smart (he had studied with Steinmetz, the socialist scientist), and he did have a great sense of humor. We were all suckers for men who could make us laff. Next to dancing, we loved laffing. So, here's this jaded dude all dressed up like a gentleman, counterpart to Margaret all dressed up like a lady. They seemed destined to meet. That's what she thought anyway. Margaret always preferred the theatrical. I liked plain everyday things. Things I could see clearly. Things I could talk about straight. But not Margaret. She needed drama. She was a dreamer. She was so down, so poor. We needed that drama too, but we didn't know it.

Margaret was also a doer. Like the time she went to Grant's to try to get a clerk's job. The manager said they didn't need her, so she picked up a five-gallon jar of yellow mustard sitting on the hot dog counter, and shouted: If you don't give me a job, I'll sling this all around. You can call the police, but you're going to have one gawdawful mess to clean up. She held the container out in front of her like a lion tamer holds a chair, then burst into tears and said, Oh, hell, set the jar down and turned to leave.

Hey, wait, the manager said. I'll take you out to lunch. And he did. And they had nice dates together almost all that summer.

That is until Neil blew back into town, just breezed in like he'd never been gone, like he'd never left her and the kids broke, homeless, holding the bag. Walked right in with that twin brother of his, Mike, talking big-shot longshoreman talk like they were big-time organizers instead of dirty little scabs like everyone knew they were. No wonder they took off so often. Anywhere they could find a strike, they'd light out for, scabbing, strike breaking. It paid a living wage in those days, same as it does now. But on Neil's first return, he met Van. And wouldn't you know it? They liked each other! You could have made book on that. Two peas in a pod, tall stories, sweet talkers, wise acres, heavy drinkers who hated women and children. They'd both say that, a la W.C. Fields. Then get a big laff. But if you knew those two, you knew they meant it. Still, I have to give them this: they really *tried* to tell us that they hated women and children. If a woman was sober and halfway paying attention, she knew where those two were coming from. Margaret was almost always sober, but she almost never paid attention in those days, like it was too painful for her. Once, when she tried to upgrade herself and took the city exam for recreationist, she got 68%. Only 68%! A smart girl like Margaret. I still shake my head over that one.

It's like talking to a wall, Nora would say, just like talking to the doggoned wall. But Nora still loved to listen to Margaret's beautiful, dreamy talk. She made everything seem possible. She made us see ourselves in ways and places we'd never thought to see ourselves. Like listening to a radio show. She'd spin a tale and make us all the stars. She enchanted us, kept us spellbound. What's she going to think of next? What's her story today?

She sometimes spoke of her father as a doctor, but she didn't like to talk about him. He was very rich and disowned her when, in the middle of college, she married Neil. I could have had anything I wanted, she said, but all I wanted was Neil. He just swept me off my feet. I must have been mad.

Other times she'd tell us her father was a big-shot judge in Houston. And she'd call him "Daddy." Daddy was a southern gentleman, raising her to be a southern lady. I can really relate to Zelda Fitzgerald, she'd say. I really can. She talked about the good-time trips to St. Loo; sailing on the Mexican Gulf; floating down the Mississippi on a paddle wheel steamer. Those were her southern belle days when she picked gardenias and wandered among the magnolias in State Capitol Park. I wandered along with her because it was a treat to be with her even when she made no sense. I used to tell her that palling around with her was cheaper than going to the movies.

Sometimes she said both her parents were college professors, taught at the same university. Then she'd say she'd attended a small Catholic college. You've never heard of it, I'm sure. Wonderful music school. That's what I studied: music. I still think of myself as a music student. On job applications and official forms, she actually wrote *Student* on the line for occupation.

And because Margaret knew so much about history and loved California history, (she would read to us from history books), you began to believe that her parents really were history professors. Margaret is the one who read Agnes Smedley's autobiography to me. I never forgot that book. Like Margaret, it changed my life, not necessarily for the better. Sometimes we groaned when Margaret cleared her throat, reached over and got out one of her books. Oh, gawd, are you going to read to us *again*?

Who else loves you enough to read aloud to you? she'd ask, eyebrows up high, cheeks sucked in. And she'd start reading because we never had an answer for that one.

Those were the days, the nights. We forgot our troubles and just listened. I remember one deathly hot summer month when we sat out every night on some broken ends of the sidewalk that Margaret called her "patio" and listened as she read from a new book about the Donner Party. Our blood ran cold. We wept and sipped our beer from tiny cheese glasses. We slumped, stunned with the misery, the courage of those people. But our spirits rose every night when we went home. She didn't have any Van or Neil around in those days. She wasn't crazy. She was her very best self.

And she was her very best self when she harangued us: Women are prisoners. When women are born, they are already in prison. Women are slaves. But her worst self acted out women as slaves. She became a slave to Neil, a slave to Van.

Van talked Margaret into putting her kids up for adoption. Van and that wild woman in Folsom who pressured her all the time. But despite all that, she continued to talk about women in ways we'd never heard. She'd read Anna Louise Strong, Agnes Smedley, Emma Goldman. She'd suddenly say, I would have been a great forest ranger. When you thought about it, she *would* have been a great forest ranger. She would have been a great lot of things. And then she'd tell us what we could do.

You ought to go to college, she said. You're fine college material.

Me, why I never even graduated from high school.

You, yes, you. You're a born student. Like me. We could both be great scholars one day.

Honest-to-gawd, Margaret, you kill me, you really do.

But as I said, I put what she said back in the very best part of my brain and thought, You know, she's right. She had the best way of spotting a person's good points, talking them up, thinking up things they could do for themselves. Like when she looked at Doris and said, You're a whiz with math. You shouldn't teach dance the rest of your life. You ought to think about math, Doris, you really should.

And here we were, envying Doris because she had her own business, worked steady. We thought she was on top of the world. But here was Margaret, who looked at the same Doris and realized a person who had talent for something long range. Doris did pride herself on her mathematical abilities but never showed it because men didn't like women who were whizzes at math.

We all talked about the usual things: going down to San Francisco, getting a job, falling in love, having a family. Even with our radical work, organizing and protesting, we still pretty much saw ourselves as marrying, giving up our social and political concerns, because that's what women were expected to do after they got married.

But Margaret talked about riding trains, talking to people, getting off in out-of-the-way places. She saw us out in the world, more in command than we saw ourselves. And you know, it was funny because here was this woman who didn't eat right, who ran around with men guaranteed to hurt her, who didn't know how to type, and who never had a good job in her life. But she just kept talking to us about going out into the world and being in command. We took her very seriously. We never laffed at her. We never knew where or how she learned to say these things. We never figured it out. We never knew.

She didn't talk in public like Nora, but she thought of things for Nora to say, things to put in speeches that would make people stop and pay attention. It was Margaret who got the idea to have the Chief of Police carry the Red Flag in the Fourth of July parade. It was Margaret who got the idea to have Nora pull a little cannon down the street, with leaflets attached on rubber bands that shot out into the crowd when Nora pulled the string.

Margaret was always filled with ideas like that. She used to say, If I could only get paid for my ideas, we'd be in clover.

The rest of us thought of one thing for all of Margaret's twenty. Sometimes it seemed her brain would never stop. But other times, with Neil and Van, it seemed it wouldn't start. Times when she felt so pressured, she couldn't pay attention, couldn't think, became vague. Not dreamy. Vague. Those were the times she drove me mad. Like, after months without a job, she went to live with Van. When she cooked, she opened cans of macaroni and cheese or spaghetti, made Jell-O in the morning instead of coffee. And when she decided to give the apartment a good cleaning, she'd get out all the cleaning rags, then lie down on the bed and read a book, not get up for hours, still clutching the rags. Sometimes, she just sat on the side of the bed, wearing her slip, one stocking half on, both feet on the floor, and stared at the wall. Those were the times she just couldn't get going, at least not until something really terrible happened. Those were the times I wanted to slap her silly. Those were the times she scared me.

And I'd think, She's going away. She's not coming back.

But she did come back and gave a laff, thought of something fun to do, a new place to go. Like the time we went down to the Union Pacific yards and asked to see the roundhouse, and they gave us a tour of the house and repair yards, treated us like visiting VIPs. Or like the day she said, I know what we'll do. We'll teach you how to play tennis!

Just like that, she gave me tennis lessons. On a private court, with a private club member's racket. I did learn how to play tennis. Imagine. Never even finished high school and there I was, running around the courts playing a good game with a woman from who knows where — Kansas City, Houston, Seattle?

Or how about the time I visited her in Roseville after she married Jimmie O'Hare and went to live in that funny house on Oak Street. She got claustrophobia up there in Roseville, missed Van, missed her pals, missed the good times out dancing. She wanted to get her kids, get her little family back together. But it just didn't work. I used to go up there to see her as often as I could. One day we plain ran out of things to say. She was leaving Jimmie soon. She was bored. Bored in that railroad town and bored with her life with Jimmie. It was a cold, drizzly, grey November day, not even the excitement of a definite rain, just steady, boring drizzle. All of a sudden she looked up from her cocoa and said, How would you like to learn to drive?

Me, drive? I'd never really thought about it. Just like that she said, I'm going to teach you how to drive. Definite, tough, she was. And I've been driving ever since, with or without a license.

But more. I remember the cold, sunny day she caught the bus to Folsom to tell her kids goodbye. She'd made up her mind to have them adopted. She told them she wouldn't see them for a long time but to remember that she loved them. Honest-to-gawd, where did she get the courage? I met her at the bus depot when she came back. I walked toward her, unable to speak. She said, Move it please. You're standing in my light. I don't know why but that made me laff. And then we talked as though we thought things would be the same again. Yet we knew they never would. Van had said over and over, I'll marry you if you get rid of those kids. That wild woman in Folsom had said, You're a lovely girl, dear, but you're a terrible mother, unfit really. There's something missing in you, something lacking. If you really love your kids, you'll give them up.

There were no day-care centers then, no child care. And that was the way people talked to women. Besides, Margaret didn't want to be a mother. Still, she didn't want *not* to be a mother. She loved those kids with all her heart. But there you are. She did it.

Five months later she broke with Van, came down with TB and landed in the hospital. She lay on her bed, face white and flat as a saucer of milk. She said, You know, you have to learn to make more demands. Start thinking of your own terms.

Can you imagine that? Margaret, Miss Utter Defeat of 1931-40. Miss Total Flop of 1931-40. Where did she get the nerve? Didn't she hear herself? What was going to happen to *her*?

When she got out of the hospital, so fragile, she landed a job as maid at the Clunie Hotel. One day as I was riding in the car of my new beau, a Mare Island sailor, I saw Margaret stepping off the curb right in front of the Capitol by the Library. I rolled down the window and shouted, Hey, Margaret! Give me a call! She smiled, nodded yes, and waved her thin, thin arm. I rolled up the window, feeling bad because I'd neglected her for months.

But the guilt was replaced by thinking that we'd meet again, and have more good times.

That was the last time I saw Margaret. I looked everywhere, asked everyone. Called the police, the hospitals, checked the obits. One day I ran into Van and asked, Where's Margaret O'Shea?

I don't know, he said. Last time I saw her she was heading for the Pacific-Greyhound depot, said she was going up to Oregon or Washington, going to stay with a brother who lived there, something like that. You tell me you don't know what's happened to Margaret? Jesus, I thought you were her best friend.

Well, there you are. That was Margaret. She just got an idea into her head and walked away. Never said goodbye. Never said boo. It's a mystery, just beats everything. Yet we never stopped talking about her, never stopped wondering. And we all loved her.

Later, those of us who knew her either moved away or were put in jail, died or were killed in the war. Some of us got caught up with something or nothing. Some of us lost touch with ourselves. Some of us prospered. Some of us didn't.

Although I went to college, just the way she said I would, now, all these years later, here I am — no job, no prospects, broke. We're in a Depression again. So I'm thinking about Margaret. Thinking about Nora. Looking for the old times, trying to regain the old days, walking the streets with holes in my pockets and holes in my shoes. But this time there's no pals, no dancing, no laffs. No place to sit out of the rain, have a cup of coffee, read the paper. No radicals around to pick up my spirits, and too poor to go wherever they are.

But still, I peer in windows, look down alleys, stare into gutters. And I think, Oh, my gawd, can it really be this bad? Once again? I shake my head saying, Yes, it's this bad. Only this time it's worse. Because I'm not young anymore, and I'm not laffing anymore. And there's no one around to teach me tennis, how to drive a car. No one to show me the dance steps. So, I'm walking through the trees by the river, shaking my head, and I'm thinking, You want Deja Vu? I'll give you Deja Vu.

The Delta in Between

The weather around there always seems hot because the land's so flat. The whole country is flat, and wide. Striped with long bands of water and long lines of trees. The country is the kind of flat that can flatten the mind. And now that smog obscures the Sierras, the eyes see nothing but flat. The hairline feels lower, the eyebrows feel lower, the eyes just naturally narrow. It is steamy. Sometimes it's hard to breathe. The steamy air means something that no one can figure out, an atmospheric-emotional mystery. One longs for that land. The soil is black. Millions of pears come from the orchards and millions of ears of corn come from the stalks. The world goes deep with life under one's feet. All life goes down deep. And like all nature-growth, it is quiet, so the land and the water are quiet with life.

Loud life comes with man, his slam-bang machinery, and his hell rides down long levee roads. Fast-loud-careless of everything, he bursts through the shine off the water and the shimmer off the land. Fast he destroys, and fast he goes.

So long dummie.

So long sucker.

Fast ride to Stockton or fast ride to hell. I just don't care. Not anymore I don't. When you've gone to the distance of speck, I'm going to climb levee banks, damm glad you've gone, and look out. Look out, way out. Or I'll bend to the ground and with my hand dig deep. I'll eat dirt and make friends with the worms. I'll lean on a limb and fall in the water. I won't come out till I've soaked up the life that is in me. Maybe I already have.

To be perfectly honest, I already have.

Who is your Mother, asks Meridel. You never talk of your Mother, she says. And I say, I don't have a Mother. I wasn't born, I was knit. *HaHaHa*. My mind goes back to the Delta. To a houseboat that rocks on the water. The sun on my face, sitting down, leaning back, eyes closed, eyelids coated and warm, eyelashes jerky then quiet, bobbing, bobbing, slipping, swaying, slipping, swaying, top water goes slap. Slap. Curling, lick, curling, lick. What kind of limbo is this? Caught between the mountains and the sea?

Margaret, honey, he said, without opening his eyes, Don't ever live like this if you can help it, between the mountains and the sea. Stuck here on flatland. Stuck here on water. And get your damm feet off the table or I'll kick them off. For gawd's sake, ain't you learned nothing? You either live in the mountains or you live on the ocean but don't live like this, right in between. The mountains pull one way, the sea pulls another, I swear it hurts. First you face one way, then another. Life seems good one way, then you long for the other. You're never satisfied. Never content. For gawd's sake, Margaret, listen to me now, dammit, you either live in the mountains or you live on the ocean. Better yet, go up near Seattle and live on the Sound with your back to the mountains like we did in 19 and 32. But don't get stuck here on this gawd-dammed Delta. Don't be stuck here when you're my age. Remember that. I know what I'm saying. You're a good kid, Margaret. I love you now go start supper.

Early Days in Acampo

By the time LaVona was born it was 1915. LaVerne was already six years old and determined that she would spend all of her time out of doors if she could. She never felt threatened by the new baby who seemed to her just like any other new baby livestock or wildlife or baby pet. LaVerne enjoyed her new sister and had only one problem of adjustment: LaVerne deeply feared that the baby was deformed, and that the grown-ups weren't facing it, that the baby was somehow "not right" (like Aunt Allie's two children) because LaVona had lived so long now on the earth without *walking*. Animals walked nearly right away after they were born, and even if you counted the fact that they had twice as many legs, a baby person spending all those months on their backs just was not right. It did not add up. This was her secret dread and when no one was around, LaVerne encouraged and bullied her baby sister with words, pokes, and pinches into making the effort to walk.

One fall afternoon she burst into tears in front of a startled company sipping on drinks on the lawn and when pressured, told that the baby who looked so perfect was actually weak, and sick, and could not walk. The grown-ups laughed, her father among them, and said in a chorus, There's nothing wrong with that baby, she's too *young* to walk. LaVerne jumped up, hurt and feverish and furious, shouting, Oh yeah? Sez who?

It was there that she got her reputation for toughness. Don't worry about Verne, her family said with considerable pride, we don't. That is one — tough — kid.

Within the family the girls were called Verne and Vona but it was insisted upon that those outside the family group call them by their full names, LaVerne and LaVona. For heaven's sake. What are names for?

Their parents, Mr. and Mrs. Minardi were melon farmers. Both had come from pioneer San Joaquin River Valley families. (Both sang and played musical instruments.) They were not rich in money but they felt the authority that comes from long-time residency and they expected the respect it was supposed to bring. They in turn gave the respect that was due to the wealthy farmers and growers and to the men of industry who brought work to the Valley, like Mr. Holt and his farm equipment factory where many of the young men worked either in growing-up jobs or else worked their whole lives, swearing that one day they would be foreman.

Mr. and Mrs. Minardi were as good as their word, and their word was their bond. They would pay their bills and prosper. They would work hard. They would wear the right clothes and say the right things. They would attend the right church. They would vote the right ticket (she was a Democrat and he was a Republican). During a crisis, when the crunch was on, when the chips were down, they would go to the aid of their neighbors. They would do the right thing. They were pillars in their community. They were the salt of the earth. They were both good-looking. They were Westerners. They were rugged individualists. They were Sons and Daughters of the Golden West, and their girls were the Apples of Their Eyes. They were their Sunshine Poppies. It is hard to imagine, therefore, the pain that Mr. Minardi felt when, many years later, and each in their turn, he had to punish his girls, then hound them from home. Banish them from his sight. Send each into exile while their mother cried softly and said, You have broken your father's heart, and then asked, Oh, how could you?

Girls, girls, girls, how could you indeed?

The Salinas Streak

Ephemeral? What's ephemeral? asked Bobo. Some kind of scented oil from plants?

Meet the Salinas Streak

I have been thinking about BoBo Minardi. BoBo Minardi was a lightweight boxer from Watsonville, California, called the "Salinas Streak." BoBo never did make good although it wasn't his fault. He left Salinas in 1962 under threat of castration, and lives now in Porterville, California, where he works in a nursing home. He never married but he tells everyone that he is a widower, and the old ladies like him. They call him "Bo," and he calls them "Hon." In the summertime BoBo wears a wide, white plastic belt and white plastic loafers. He wears a ring that he recently bought in a pawn shop in Visalia. BoBo learned to waterski three summers ago and considers himself "fit as a fiddle" although the teenage girls at Lake Success do not agree. He joined a local Pentecostal church last Christmas Eve called the Nine Golden Doors, and he will vote for the first time in his life in the 1984 elections. (BoBo returned to Watsonville to have Thanksgiving dinner with his favorite uncle's ex-wife, and no one remembered who he was. Early the next morning, he robbed and beat an old lady before uprooting every plant in her garden. He is heartily sorry for that act, and will never do anything like that again.) In 1951, BoBo was voted "Biggest Little Prick at Watsonville High" but he doesn't know that. BoBo's real name is FitzHugh. FitzHugh Minardi.

BoBo's mother, LaVona, went to visit her aunt in Fresno, California, in the summer of 1933. She had grown up outside of Acampo, and had just graduated from Manteca High. After the summer was over she planned to return to Acampo to marry Chester Lytell even though he was still a married man. While visiting her aunt, LaVona and her two cousins went to the Fourth of July picnic and dance where she spent the entire evening dancing with a typewriter repairman who told her that his name was Terry FitzHugh. Instead of driving her home after the dance like he promised, he drove her due south, and four miles northwest of Goshen he pulled the car to a stop and raped LaVona Minardi, the fastest typist in her class, not once but twice. (Later, Terry, whom his family described as an Irish Jack London, would laff and wink at the Fresno Chief of Police and say—Are you kidding? She *loved* it.)

LaVona was sent to live with her divorced sister in Salinas. When she did marry it was to an old man named Charlie Osling who owned the ReddiRight Dry Cleaners chain and spit up jade green phlegm four or five times a day. (Nora says that you know the true story of Charlie Osling and how he got to be so callous and so careless so young.) The town's parents called him "Old Man Osling." Their children called him "Old Turkey Turds." LaVona seldom made eye contact with BoBo during the years when he was growing up. When she did view BoBo full-face and straight-on, it was with the same dumb surprise with which she beheld Terry FitzHugh when he turned to her in the dark car and said: Okay, Kid, let's have it.

BoBo continues to write to LaVona after all these years even though she never writes back. After reading his letters, LaVona puts them in an old Robert Hall suit box that she keeps under the bed.

There Is Something about BoBo

The reason that I said that I don't even *think* about BoBo anymore is that I don't. I don't think about him because I don't want to think about him. It makes me feel bad. First I am mad at him, then I feel sorry for him. Back and forth. Back and forth. It gives me a pain. Is that why I am always mad at BoBo? Because I feel sorry for him? Is it because I feel that he's hopeless? *He* doesn't think he's hopeless. At least I don't think that he does. He's got his "own little life." He doesn't complain. (He never did complain. He never did anything right, and he never complained.) Geeze, BoBo gives me the pip. The little twerp. That's it—that's what makes me so dammed mad—*I've got a soft spot for BoBo!*

Gawd, Lord, what next? Third stage syphilis maybe. *HaHaHa*. No, no, no, I am not going to tell you something corny like BoBo used to come down and sweep up at the store every day after school. The times of the year when he lived in Watsonville, he had to work after school for his stepdad, Turkey Turds Osling. (Whew, that man was a wreck. He had a body like something blown off the back of a garbage truck. *HaHa*.) What *I* used to pay BoBo to do was to go get me a beer and cigarettes late at night or when it was cold and I didn't want to go out. But he used to like to come to the store anyway and read the mags, and look at the jewelry, and show me the things that he thought his Mom would like, and try on the clothes made out of soft, old stuff. (I owned and ran the best secondhand clothes and misc. store in Watsonville, for almost twenty years. The Wee Bonnie Thrift. J stands for Jo Johannsen, Prop. As a matter of fact, I was the first woman ever to be nominated to the Watsonville Businessmen's Club, or so they tell me, which isn't only a matter of fact, but also a matter of a lot of bouncy-bouncy with Your Honor, The Mayor — one of "Jo's Boys."*HaHaHa*. I didn't ever belong but at least I got nominated.)

BoBo never bothered me then like he bothers me now. He never bothered me then at all. I liked him. He was a nice kid. Clean. Nice manners. I liked him but I know a lot of them who didn't. I'm not sure why. (And you can forget that deal with Helen Buck and her Dad. Tommy Buck didn't know left from right. He never did.) There was just *something* about BoBo. Something you just wanted to stomp on — like some dammed bug.

And no. For the five-hundredth time, no. I don't *want* you to come over, and yes, I've been drinking, and no, I'm not *drunk*. I just wish I'd been nicer to the little guy, that's all.

Love Drives

BoBo was madly in love. He had been for quite some time. She's My True Love, he thought. This is it. At last I've found her. The girl of my dreams. His friend Lou said, BoBo, you're nuts. She wouldn't give you the time of day. She doesn't even know you're alive.

True, it took almost a year before she returned one of his smiles. Or gave him a nod. Or presented one word that acknowledged his humanness, his aliveness, his nearness. But one night, for no apparent reason, she said, Oh yeah. Hello. BoBo, is it? and kept on walking back to the table with the good-lookers, the good-dancers, the good-dressers, the good-laffers. A place where he'd never sit down.

It was the morning after that night that he fell in love. Her words went through his head for weeks. He was like someone hallucinating, wrapped and cushioned in love. Happy and warm with words no one else could hear. He was the winning spinner of the lucky wheel. He stopped eating. I don't need food, he told Lou, I can live on her words. You're a dammed fool, said his friend. You gotta eat. You gotta eat to live. I'm living on love, said BoBo. One day he fainted at work. The foreman stood over him and snapped, You look like hell! Are you sure you can handle this job? Oh, that made BoBo mad. He'd been doing an excellent job for a long time now. What nerve! Who'd that guy think he was talking to anyway? But it scared him so he started to eat again.

The object of BoBo's affections was a pretty and complex young woman named Nadine. Newly divorced Nadine. A young woman with far too much time on her hands. She didn't work at a steady job. No need. She had alimony. The only woman in town who ever had alimony. It made some men dammed mad. Angry and fearful of the feelings that she aroused in them. It made some women mad too, for they also struggled with feelings of fear and fury. But no one criticized out loud. At least not in public. Not in Manteca anyway. No one dared. You just did not speak loosely about Tom's daughter, Nadine. Lovely, perky, with the highest heels in the county and the longest nails until she broke them all in a jitterbug contest over in Oakland. No sir, you better not speak badly about Nadine. Why, if anyone puts this town on the map, it's gonna be that Nadine or her Dad, they nodded to one another over the Businessmen's Lunch at the Downtown Cafe. Tom was old-family. A small realtor-developer. But successful. On his way to the bigtime. Folks in the Capitol were beginning to notice the whys and wherefores of this local boy. And his daughter, Nadine? Now there was a girl to warm the cockles of the heart of every Dad in California. Shantung Nadine. Who danced like Rita Hayworth, and, some said, looked like her too.

Now Nadine had no car. Behind closed doors where no one could hear, Tom told her, No, dammit, Nadine, I'm not buying you one more stinking dammed thing. That's final. The young men and women she knew were either in college or working all day so she was trapped in town, and the days got longer than she cared to admit. She got downright bored. None of her pals would lend her their cars either, not since that bloody accident she had up above Jackson. Dammed near killed her. Smashed Dan's car, smashed her body. It took ages to heal. It wasn't my fault. It wasn't my fault. True, she'd been blinded by drunken tears of self-pity, crippled with the pain of that night's rejection by that lousy guy who ran the Firestone agency. I don't know what I saw in him anyway. Married too. Just who did he think he was, anyway? (I never date married men, she told her friends. I'm firm in that. She meant it too, never counting the several married men she had affairs with over the years. They didn't matter. Just because she dated *them* it didn't mean that it was her *policy* to date married men. She was very firm about that.) What she saw in that lousy guy was his route that took him all over the Valley, up into the Sierras, and sometimes out to the coast. Why they could drive up to Ft. Bragg and back, have sex along the way, and be back in town not much past midnight, with no one the wiser. That's my kind of living, she thought. I could drive forever.

So when BoBo saved enough from his cannery job in Stockton to buy that blue Plymouth coupe, Nadine looked up, and took notice. You're not thinking of dating BoBo? asked her friend, Betty. You can't be. Why not? Why shouldn't I? I've dated lots worse.

For the next eight months they went for drives. At first once a month. Then once a week. Nadine got so she really liked the little guy. He never tried to interfere in her real life. She liked that. It meant he knew his place. And he was always ready to go. At the drop of a hat. Feel like going for a drive? she'd ask. And he'd say, I'm game. Where to?

They never talked much as they drove. When there was talk, it was mostly Nadine's. He'd laugh when she did, and twice he made what Nadine considered a joke. There, she thought, I knew there was more to him than meets the eye. She came to count on the drives. Him with both hands on the wheel, her with her face to the wind.

He drove where she said to drive and stopped when she told him to. Then started home when she said it was time. It was all getting dreamy and rather nice. He bought her cherry Cokes in Placerville, and thought, I'm yours, Nadine. Greek Goddess from Manteca. I'm yours for life.

Oh, he knew she dated other men. And it was okay with him if she refused to be seen with him in public except when they were sitting in his car. That didn't matter to BoBo. Because what they had was special. Like when poetry rhymes. These drives with Nadine were everything he'd prayed for, more than he'd prayed for. It was heaven. "Heaven above knows your my true love." He'd hum, and imagine him and Nadine dancing on a black ballroom floor, just like Fred and Ginger. Twirling. Stepping. Sliding. Eyes locked. Arms locked. Twirling and gliding. The world somewhere over to the side, too respectful to intrude. No, BoBo had no complaints. Not until October when he began to have sex fantasies he felt he might not be able to control. A couple of times he got a hard-on at work. The guys laffed and called him Little Big Horny and BangBang. He went to confession. He got down on his knees and prayed. He took cold showers. But whenever they drove by a motel somewhere, anywhere, BoBo almost passed out from desire. Once, passing the DingDong Motel in Fresno, he lost control of the car. What's the matter with you? screamed Nadine. My gawd, what'er you trying to do? Kill me?

BoBo swung the car to the curb. His face dropped to his hands and he started to cry. Kill you? he blubbered. Kill you? Oh, my gawd! He wept big shoulder-shaking, jaw-wrenching sobs. His eyes ran with tears. His nose clogged with snot. Stop crying! Stop crying, for Pete's sake! Someone will hear you. Look, I can't stand it. Nadine put her arms around BoBo, something she swore she'd never do, and let him fondle her right breast right there in the middle of the day, not far from downtown Fresno. Put your hand on me. Please, he begged, his nose at her throat. Put your hand on me. Do it. Nadine laughed gently and sat back against the door. You're so sweet, BoBo, you really are. Now let's go.

BoBo didn't see Nadine for a full six weeks. He felt too ashamed. Too coarse. Too vulgar. Too unworthy. I don't deserve the love of a woman like her, he swore to his friend, Lou, who said, You know, I worry about you. In the seventh week, Nadine called and said, Come on, let's go for a drive to Ione.

They drove to the Capitol, and ate lunch in the park. They drove to Carmel, and walked on the sand. They drove to the City and fed gulls on the wharf. The expense is killing me, thought BoBo, but it's worth it.

On a sunny day late in May Nadine called and asked, Can I borrow the car? He was surprised. You know I wouldn't ask if it wasn't important, she said. I'm sure you know that. Here, he said, when she came for the keys, I won't even ask where you're going. Oh, what a doll, she said, kissing him on the cheek. You're a living doll.

That's the last BoBo saw of Nadine. She sent him a postcard from Reno with a picture of the Mapes Hotel. The message read: Hi! Married yesterday. Thanks for the car. It's in the hotel garage. Can you pick it up? Flying to Miami. Wish me luck? N. xxoo

BoBo went into decline and collapsed. He was caught in fits of coughing and crying that he swore he couldn't control. Lou went to Reno and brought back the car. The landlady said, Look Kid, you're beginning to give me the creeps. Lou said, Come on, BoBo, face it. She never cared for you. Shape up. Get up. But BoBo was determined. He swore that the only way they would ever get him out of his room was to carry him out feet first. Which they did. Wrapped tight in a blanket, they transported him to the State Hospital in Stockton where he stayed drugged for three months.

Upon his release, BoBo gave his car keys and pink slip to Lou. Here, Lou, it's all yours. What a pal, beamed Lou. Are you sure? Oh, I'm sure, all right. I never want to drive that car again. Hurts too much. Reminds me of her. Reminds me of our days of love. Oh, don't worry. I'm over it now. I'm almost well. My thoughts are clear. Don't worry your head about me. I've come through it all right. Though my heart is broken in a million pieces, I'm gonna live. Because you know, Lou? BoBo's lips began to tremble. It's better to have loved and lost than never to have loved at all.

Oh, for crissakes, BoBo, said his best friend Lou. Wise up.

Heart Wattle

It really hurts to be called a bum. You guys don't know that but it does, BoBo cried with steamy tears and watery snot running out his nose, onto the sides of his mouth and down off his chin. His fists clenched white at his sides and it was all he could do to keep from punching himself. Someday you guys will be laughing out of the back of your mouths, he prophesied.

Go on, get outta here, BoBo, before we sell you to the gypsies.

For years Bobo had known that he had to be punished. He kept remembering the way he had beat up that old lady and ruined her garden. He felt ashamed and sad. The memory of that crime made a heavy lump in his mind, a heavy lump burning on his heart. He wanted to be punished, once and for all, so he could get rid of that feeling, and so he went to the Watsonville police station to turn himself in.

He didn't want to go to jail but he secretly hoped that the cops would beat him up for his crime. All they did was laugh. We don't want to listen to any of your fruitcake confessions, they said.

They were nothing, he thought, nothing but big meanies with big guns. Public servants too. And here he was, a taxpayer. Hey, who do you think pays your salary? Damm, he wished he'd said that. But they'd have just laughed more. Maybe he should go to the Mayor's office and complain. But why bother? The whole thing had turned out wrong.

Earlier, he'd gone to the old lady's house to beg for forgiveness and offer his yard services for the rest of his life. But the neighbors said that she'd died a couple of years ago. And, no, she didn't have any relatives. The house had gone to the state.

Cheeze Whiz, if I'd come sooner she might've left me her house out of gratitude for being her last friend. Her last helper. He could have run errands for her, heated up soup. Damm. What crummy luck.

So, what next? The state didn't want vengeance. There were no relatives to take vengeance. BoBo, it seemed, was on his own. He bought a bag of Cheetos, a package of DingDongs, two Cokes and went to the beach. I always think better at the beach, he told himself. It's the salt water, I'll bet.

Leaning back against a charred log, he tried to figure out how he could punish himself for his crime and end his misery. Let's see. Maybe I could stab myself. But he was afraid of infections. It could lead to gangrene. I could pinch a hunk of flesh on my thigh with pliers until my eyes watered. But, there again, the danger of infection and gangrene. Well, hell. I could drop a big rock on my foot, but I have to walk, don't I? He couldn't afford to sit around with his foot propped up on some lousy pillow. He was a working man. Maybe I could go to one of those terrifying, sicko movies and scare myself silly. But he didn't want to poison his mind or go nuts. That stuff could scar a person for life, make them go off the deep end and never come back.

Shooting himself was out. He didn't own a gun and was afraid to buy one. (They did those mental health checks.) And besides, think of the noise! He didn't want to go deaf, for crying out loud. What if I got a big stick and hit myself around the body and legs, hard enough to hurt, but not hard enough to cripple myself. He didn't want to have to push himself around in a wheel chair or use crutches like he had to that time he fell down the stairs. What a painful experience that was. He thought about burning himself but, Lord, no, think of the smell. Whewee. No thanks. Leave that to G. Gordon Liddy. What, oh what, was he to do?

What if he climbed to the top of a high, rocky hill, lay down with his arms folded, and rolled all the way to the bottom? That's a good one. Wow, he liked that. But the good feeling faded as he thought about the dangers awaiting him along the way: an angry mother rattlesnake, nettles from some poisonous plant, putting his eyes out on a sudden sharp rock. Better forget that one. Too bad.

Too bad is right. Too bad that people who want to do right, can't. There's people in this world who never even think about justice. There's people in this world who just laugh at the idea of penance. But not this kid. I think about it all the time. I want to do justice. I want to do penance.

Most of all, he wanted to get rid of that itchy, lumpy thing on his brain, that heavy, hanging thing on his heart. BoBo stood up, stepping on the only blossoming plant on the beach. He wiped the greasy crumbs and sand from his hands onto his pants. He buttoned his coat. Wearing this thing that hangs on my heart, he thought, maybe that's my punishment. Tears came to his eyes. Okay, he said, okay. I'll wear it till I die. Just see if I don't.

BoBo's Christmas BooBoo

Have you heard the news? BoBo is working the Valley, from Redding to Bakersfield, as a faith healer. What next! His working the last ten years in old folks' homes plus what we now laffingly call The Christmas Miracle (Danny is still far from laffing), seem to have brought BoBo to his new profession. To what he now considers his Mission in life. Or as BoBo says with chin all aquiver — what I was *born* for. So do you laff or do you cry? One of the reasons that BoBo is such a dammed nuisance to know is that you're always caught on the grating edge of laffter or tears, uncomfortable with the conflict and resentful of the source of irritation. But you could put BoBo in a vacuum and he'd still be a pain in the ass. Anyway, here's what happened:

All the gang from Bryte and Broderick, myself and my steady, plus Cosmo (with his sinus packed) and the folks from San Joaquin were going to spend two days during Christmas week with Trees on his houseboat in the Delta. One evening we planned to go up and down the river singing carols and visiting with some of R. Louie's and Sam's and Trees's old pals who can't get out so easy anymore. This included a visit with Danny Delta, once billed as "Danny Delta, the Fighting Irishman, Rio Vista's Own," until his accident. We planned to stop at the bridge in RV while some of the guys from the Paddle Wheel Cafe pushed Danny's chair down to the river so that we could toast him, sing to him, and all around let him know that there are still plenty of folks outside of Rio Vista who think he's hot stuff. His twenty years out of sight doesn't mean twenty years out of mind. Bones

Maroni wrote a verse he was going to set to music but didn't, so we were just going to recite it:

With glasses raised on high
With faces to the sky,
We salute one hell of a guy
Who fought and deserves
His fame.
Fighting Danny Delta is his name.
Hoo. Ray.

On the afternoon of the 23rd we were all there, floating from Frank's Dock toward Rio Vista and the bridge. FayAnn was there with Hal and flirting with Sam per usual. Consuelo was there. She didn't want to spend the night so she drove down alone. Jimmie Sue refused to come at all. You must think I'm some kind of fool. Those Delta crackers hang people like me from their Christmas trees. I don't know where she got this kind of information but she couldn't be budged. Ben and Dixie were there. Sawyer Lee was there. In other words, everyone we considered anyone was there that day. We were having a good old rip-roaring time—drinking, eating, telling whoppers, playing cards, dancing, swapping jokes, all wearing our Mae Wests so there'd be no sweat if someone fell overboard. But perfection was seriously flawed when BoBo came uninvited. From somewhere. How he got from Lodi to the boat is known to God alone because *we* sure didn't know. No one there would have driven one mile to pick up BoBo, let alone driven all the way to Lodi where he got off the bus. But there he was. And not so bad that day either. Doing pretty good in fact. Being kind of quiet, pretty much keeping to himself. Making himself useful too. Pouring drinks, making fancy little sandwiches that

Trees called Pansy Crap, mixing drinks, and emptying ashtrays.

The closer we got to the bridge the more we talked about Danny. Everyone told how they'd first met him, where they'd seen him last, and wasn't his luck a dammed lousy shame. And there he sat with six big hurly-burlies from Danny's fan club standing by his wheelchair on the bank. Two of the guys held the door from the men's bathroom at the Shell station, and when we were positioned right, threw it down. With a lot of bouncing and some buckling, they rolled the Fighting Irishman on board. Only spiny cacti would have failed to have been moved by the next hour—everyone kissing, back slapping, hugging, play-punching. A lot of good cheer, a lot of good feelings. Everyone just head over heels in love with everyone else is about the best way to describe it. Till trouble came. Trouble named You Know Who. BoBo, who'd been hopping around, hovering on the outside of the group where he belonged, suddenly pushed to the front, tears on his face and his arms outstretched, looking to one and all like he was about to give Danny the hug of his life. Danny saw him coming and screamed, Get back! Get back! That didn't stop BoBo. Danny swung both fists into the air, jumped up out of that chair, shouting, Don't touch me you creep, and ran stumbling and staggering back up the hill to the center of town, a guy who hadn't walked in the last twenty years.

Clasping his skinny little hands to his chest, BoBo dropped to his knees and sobbed, I healed him, Lord, didn't I? I healed him. We just stood there aghast, holding our drinks, holding our cards, holding our partners, our mouths dropped open. Stanley Lamponi jumped overboard shouting, Forgive me, Jesus. The five guys from the Paddle Wheel Cafe came to, and ran up the hill after Danny who, it turned out, with all the luck of the Irish, ran smack into the new Deputy Sheriff just coming off his dinner hour. One of these hot shot college kids who thinks he knows the secrets of the universe after two semesters of psychology. He arrested Danny for disturbing the peace and Danny called him a dumb you-know-what then passed out at the Deputy's feet. So now Danny is sitting out the New Year in County Jail in spite of the public outcry. Danny has sworn revenge but BoBo doesn't know anything about that because he's riding up and down the damm Valley, wearing his white plastic shoes and his wide, white plastic belt, healing the sick with Stanley Lamponi who dried himself off and offered his services as BoBo's chauffeur and bodyguard. The doctor in Stockton says that Danny could have walked years ago if he'd wanted to. But with so many guys knocking each other down for the chance to wait on him, why should he? Danny's doctor in Rio Vista, who's also deacon at the Church of the Holy Reformed, says that's rot. He's certain that Danny had a true and bona fide miracle. He's talking to his church about it now, and they've notified headquarters in Tennessee.

One thing is for certain. That guy BoBo is making money hand over fist.

Good Elements

Could you have known Consuelo and never have told a soul?

Good Elements

Meet my friend and sometimes colleague, a short-order cook from Galveston by way of Oklahoma City and Missouri, a little French guy named Ratouie Louie. He's a skinny little guy, a onetime heavy smoker with a nonproductive cough, who has sharp little teeth, narrow elbows, and wears pointed shoes. A hell of a swell guy with a hell of a swell smile, and he knows all the tricks or a lot of them anyway. A good guy to have on your side. He likes a good story and can tell a few himself. I first met him when he was cooking for Dixie at the Drop Anchor Inn off of Jefferson. He came to my aid in that nasty fight we had out in Bryte over passing out handbills door-to-door, and then again in Broderick when we were fighting city hall over the eviction of the trailer court folks down there on 5th Street who have lived in that park since before you and I were a gleam in our parents' eyes. I'm telling you, he's a guy who really knows how to go for the throat. I get to laffing just thinking about it.

And here's something that's going to give you a jolt; R. Louie knew Neil and Mike before Neil married Margaret and they came to California. He knew them when they were scabbing in Houston before R. Louie joined the Wobblies. He met them one morning at a hiring hall and then ran into them again in Washington doing WPA jobs on the Bonneville Dam project. Some small world, huh? That eyeball that's tattooed in the middle of his forehead made me awful nervous when I first knew him. But you get used to it. R. Louie never mentions it (maybe he's forgot it's there), so I don't either. He used to have a certain reputation for meanness so maybe, well, I don't know.

I just figure when he wants to let me know what it signifies he'll let me know. But don't get me wrong. R. Louie is not a hooligan. He grows flowers in those big restaurant cans. Nasturtiums, all colors, orange, red, yellow, pink, you name it, all those hot colors, hot like the sun. He not only grows them — he eats them. I'm not kidding. He eats them. He made us a salad once, and threw some of those nasturtiums in the bowl (Nasty Urchins, he calls them), and we ate them with our lunch. They were good too. I'm telling you, R. Louie knows all the tricks.

I figure that R. Louie is at least seventy, but he doesn't look a day over fifty-five. And that's just one of the reasons why we were all so surprised when that good-looking young woman came to town carrying a suitcase in one hand and a hat box in the other. She disappeared inside R. Louie's bungalow for three days. We didn't see Louie for five days and never did see her again. She was a good looker, and a good dresser too. I wish I'd had the nerve to ask her name. R. Louie has a bungalow on Dixie and Ben's two acres. It's old and not very big, but he's fixed it up real nice and I always like going over there to visit. I like to sit on the front porch and play solitaire and listen to R. Louie and Jimmie Sue swap stories about working in the shipyards during World War II. Louie cooked in Richmond, and then at Marinship in Sausalito which is where he met Jimmie Sue who was just out from Georgia with her three kids, her mother, and her five brothers. They all worked the shipyards at one time or another. Jimmie Sue lives in one of the old migrant workers' shacks a half block from the River and twenty feet below the levee road. She's lived there for twenty-five years. The only house she goes into other than her own is Ratouie Louie's. She hardly gives me the time of day but I like her anyway. Jimmie Sue has worked as a cleaning woman at the Capitol for years now and could afford to live in a much nicer place but she likes it where she is. She says it reminds her of Georgia. Jimmie Sue must have a bundle of money by now but nobody ever sees it, and she doesn't talk about it. I don't know what ever happened to her family. Nobody ever sees them either.

One of R. Louie's best friends is Sam the Sign Painter. Sam used to paint signs for the big movie companies but he hit the skids somehow, recovered, and now lives the quiet life but still paints signs from time to time. He does real special work and gets a big fee when he asks for it. I am more than fond of Sam, and I like to spend as much time with him as I can. Sam says that he's in love with me but that he is too old for me sexually so we never had an affair. But we're best friends and spend a lot of time together. Sam is the only man who ever spoke straight out to me about sex, and it embarrassed me terribly. For the past two summers R. Louie and I have had concessions at the Yolo and Placer County fairs, real nice food booths. Sam painted the signs for us "on the house." So Sam eats with us "on the house." When Theodora Bloxx, the Great Women's Writer, came to town, Sam painted a beautiful sign that said WELCOME TO THEODORA BLOXX, and we stretched it across 6th Street so that when Sawyer brought her home he had to drive right through it. It was a real thrill. We lined up on the side of the street and waved and cheered when they drove by. She stayed at Esstell and Sawyer's for almost a week. R. Louie cooked a big spaghetti dinner in her honor, with special wine, and people came from all over to meet her and listen to her stories about union organizing in the Thirties and women in The Great Depression. Jimmie Sue says that we are all on the FBI list now but it was worth it just to be around Theodora for all that time and listen to her talk. We still write to one another. We're probably all on the FBI list now anyway with all the work we do resisting The System. R. Louie has been resisting and organizing and fighting for years now, just like about everyone else I know. He's been in a lot of fights, some he won't talk about. He's little but he's a fighter. Like I said before, he has a certain reputation for meanness.

Twice a year, once in the spring and once in the fall, R. Louie and Sam go down the Delta and rent a houseboat and fish and talk and read for a week. Sometimes Hal and I go along. I hate it but Hal loves it. We've been dating for about six years now. He is a real nice guy and popular too. A lot of folks say that he will be mayor of the town one of these days. We have a lot of fun and like to go dancing. Hal's never rude to my friends but in private he calls them The Menagerie. He likes to get me away from The Menagerie, he says. Sometimes we go away for the weekend. I say that I'm going to spend the weekend with Consuelo, and then Hal and I meet somewhere. Consuelo says that I'm crazy if I marry him but Consuelo is always shooting her mouth off about something. I tell her so too. She has a darling house out in Bryte with honeysuckle and baby's breath growing over the front porch and a bird bath in the middle of the backyard lawn. Consuelo has waitressed at the El Rancho for years, through the good times and the bad, and she brings home fabulous tips. She takes real good care of herself and her house. Consuelo says she lives single because she hasn't met anyone good enough for her, but the truth is she's been married twice already and has two kids who live with their father down in Dago. Consuelo is full of a lot of beautiful beans but you couldn't ask for a better friend. She and R. Louie don't hit it off though. They fight like cats and dogs. They got into a real donnybrook at my last birthday party, and she ended up throwing a dish of ice cream at R. Louie, which sent Sam and me into screams of hysterics, laffing and hanging onto one another. That made Hal sore and he got up and stomped out. Jimmie Sue took out after Consuelo, throwing hunks of French bread at her and shouting all kinds of southern curses. We had a wonderful time, and I just love thinking about it. I wish you could have been there. You'd have died laffing. R. Louie wouldn't speak to Consuelo for weeks afterwards because the ice cream she threw was Neapolitan and the combination made a stain that wouldn't come out. R. Louie is real particular about his clothes. When he cooks he wears berets, little neck scarves, and striped t-shirts. When he dresses up he wears turtlenecks and tweeds and linens that look real good on his skinny frame. The truth is, he is one good-looking man. He says that he's one-third Choctaw, one-third African, one-third French, and one-third Irish. I can't figure that one out but he must know what he's talking about—it's *his* blood.

Sam and R. Louie are off to Folsom on a mysterious errand this afternoon so I'm in charge of watering the garden. Right now I'm just lying here in the hammock under the mock locust trees, staring up at the sky through my eyelashes. Last week some battle-axe told a reporter from the *Sacramento Bee* that Louie LaDoux and his friends were "a bad element in East Yolo County." But she's full of beans. We're good elements. Maybe just a little too loud.

Justice for Consuelo

Today is Saturday. It's Saturday afternoon. Three weeks ago to the day, Consuelo was beaten up on her own front lawn. Mr. French said that she should be thankful she wasn't raped too. That made R. Louie so dammed mad he threw Mr. French out of the diner, and told him that if he heard any more remarks like that about gratitude that Mr. French would be wearing his teeth in his hip pocket. Consuelo had been robbed about ten days before the beating, and she told the cops that she thought the job had been done by the four young punks who had moved into the neighborhood a little while before. They had been causing a lot of trouble. There had been robberies in blocks of houses that had never been robbed before. So when Consuelo got home late that night there they were sitting on the lawn and the first thing that they said to her was — You reported us to the police, bitch.

Consuelo told them to get the hell off her front lawn, that she wasn't afraid of them, that they were nothing but cheap punks, that she hoped their balls dropped off. They couldn't make her beg, and they couldn't make her cry so they broke her nose, blacked her eyes, knocked her front teeth out, and damaged both her shoulders.

Well, you can imagine. We have been sick and angry. We are sad and we are serious, and we are filled with anger. No arrests were made and the cops said that the guys disappeared. Thanks for nothing. Consuelo just lies there not looking like herself and not saying much, all bruised and damaged and full of pain. She's been quiet as a mouse, and frankly, I'm worried.

I always carry a knife but Consuelo never armed herself with anything. She used to laff and say that she would just shoot off her big mouth and her attacker would fall dead at her feet. Very funny. It didn't work out that way. But I'm glad she shot her mouth off anyway. I'm not one of those people who think that women should be quiet and polite while they are being attacked. Not me. Not most people I know either. I just wish Consuelo had at least carried a little knife. Or even a rock. Well, that's in the past now. What isn't in the past is how we're going to handle this terrible thing. R. Louie says we are just going to keep calm and handle it the way we usually handle these terrible things. Sam seconds that. We all do. It's just that it's hard to keep calm when you see your beautiful friend lying there all smashed and battered. But cold and calm is the only way to go is what I'm fast learning.

Marge's youngest nephew is a Sacramento County deputy sheriff, and he says that one of the punks is hiding out in South Sacramento; one is hiding out in Del Paso Heights; and one is living right downtown near the Greyhound Bus terminal at 7th and L. Punk Number Four hasn't been found yet. So.

I am in.

R. Louie is in.

Sam is in.

Jimmie Sue is staying with Consuelo at R. Louie's place.

Bones Maroni is in.

Hal is out.

Cosmo is out.

Sawyer Lee would be in but his heart is not good these days.

Marge is in.

Sacto Ruth would be in but she has to work.

Esstell Lee is in.

When Tough Tony Swanetti heard about the beating he went a little crazy so R. Louie got him drunk and has him stashed up in Jackson. I wouldn't want him in anyway, the creep.

Night Tire will be here soon, and he's in.

So tonight, when it's dark, we will meet where we always meet. We will wear our black clothes. We will be calm. We will be organized and we will get justice for Consuelo.

As my dear old Daddy used to say, Three outta four, ain't bad. It ain't bad at all.

Consuelo Loves Night Tire

For all her pretty ways, Consuelo was tough. Tough as hide. When all reasonable arguments failed, she wasn't shy to get up close and yell. She knew how to shoot a hand gun although she didn't own one. She knew how to throw a punch, how to kick, gouge, and scratch. But she seldom did. Rarely in her life did she get mean and physical because mostly she got by on her attitude. Consuelo had a very commanding way. She earned people's respect just by the way she walked. She knew how to stand up straight, how to carry herself in a way that said she knew who she was and where she was going, which was exactly the case. She used to say, I'm very self-assured. Amen to that, we'd say.

It was this very self-assurance that first attracted Night Tire to her. Night Tire (so-called because he owned and operated the most successful nighttime rolling security outfit in the state of Nevada) was a lawyer who didn't practice law but gave advice freely. He gave up law because he wanted to dress the way he felt like it on any particular day and because he wasn't pleased with the criminal justice system the way his peers thought he ought to be. So, screw it, said Night Tire, and got himself the big money security operation that a lot of us thought was the next best thing to being a movie star.

Consuelo never dated guys who weren't critical thinkers. She never dated guys who smoked or drank, a point of view that seriously limited the field. But Consuelo was patient. I can wait, she'd say. And we knew she could. She was that kind of person. She had her standards and she knew who she was. She didn't rush things because she didn't have a lot of doubts. So Night Tire fit right in with her idea of a good man who would show her a good time. He felt the same about her.

Between her waitress job and his security business they didn't get to be together but once a month, sometimes less. I can wait, she'd say. Consuelo wasn't the kind of person to run after anything less than what she really wanted. Lonely? she'd say. Sure, sometimes I get lonely. So what. Lonely doesn't last. Bad feelings last. Bad moves last. Not lonely.

Consuelo and Night Tire have been involved with one another for almost five years now. But don't look for a wedding soon. Consuelo lives single. She doesn't really believe in marriage for women. Same goes for Night Tire. They have the same idea: they plan to wed when they're in their seventies. They plan to marry old so they can be last lovers, last companions, last friends. She really cares for this guy. You can see that he feels deeply about her too.

We all like him a lot. Although we suspect that he doesn't take to us as gladly as we think he ought to. It's too bad. He's really a great guy. We love the way he makes Consuelo happy. It's just that sometimes we make him nervous. Some of our best plans make him turn pale and that always gives us a big laff. Consuelo says, Don't worry about it. Our trouble is, we're too ahead of our time.

It's the American Way

Charlie and Violet have been gone for over two weeks now. Ratouie Louie says that while they shaved at least ten years off his life, he wouldn't have missed them for the world. Sam the Sign Painter says, Thank gawd, that's over. Jimmie Sue says that anybody who can get themselves lost in Broderick, California, oughtn't be allowed to walk around loose, and that's just for starters. Hal says that someday we'll all look back on this and laff. (Tony Swanetti says, Hey, what happened to the loonies?) Bones Maroni says that he's going to put the whole thing to music. Consuelo says, What a couple of dingbats. Me, I don't know what to say. Sure they were pretty wild but they were pretty all right too. In their way. If I had to say anything, I'd say I'm amused and confused.

Don't believe what you read in the papers about Charlie and Violet either. At least don't believe a lot of it. For instance, there are a lot of strange stories being written about where they came from. I *still* don't know exactly where they came from but I do know how they got here. Cause I was there.

It was a warm and sunny Sunday. We were all sitting around in the garden in back of R. Louie's place. Just smelling the leaves after the rain, watching the daffodils, hyacinths, and narcissus bursting to bloom. Hearing the soft sounds of a day-off afternoon. Just drifting and dreaming. Enjoying our own company. Before you know it, Wham! The cat jumped up hissing and meowing, arching it's back, and ran under the porch. The dogs started whining and barking and ran to the fence in the back. What a commotion! We heard someone saying, Nice doggie, nice doggie. Then, forcing their way through the underbrush, ivy hanging from their knees, came two of the strangest looking people I had ever seen. Don't get up, said the man. You're Ratouie Louie, just the man we've come to see. I'm Charlie and this is Violet. Don't call her Vi. Sorry we scared you like that but we got lost. They turned to each of us with wide, happy smiles, and although their skins were white as snow, they gave Jimmie Sue the Black Power clenched fist salute and said, Hello there, Sister! We sat glued to our seats.

Both had black hair. Violet's was stiff like straw but Charlie's was curly like a poodle's. They were dressed all in black from head to foot. Tight black t-shirts, creased black jeans, black narrow sunglasses, and on their feet shiny black Wellington boots. Each carried a black satchel that looked like an old-time medical bag, Fair Play for Cuba stickers stuck on one side and yellow and black Have a Happy Day faces painted on the other. Around their waists they wore belts of link chain. Our love chains, they called them. We're chained in love. Still standing, they explained that they had sought out R. Louie and his friends for help. They were here, they said, to organize and put into motion the First National Nuke Puke. It was something they wanted to be real dramatic, real ugly, just like the ugly of getting nuked. Go see R. Louie everyone had said.

I'm going home, said Jimmie Sue, I got a real big headache. And she got up and left. I'd better go with her, make sure she's got aspirin, said Bones Maroni, and he got up and left. Well, I've got some paperwork to catch up on, said Hal, and he got up and left.

Don't leave *me* here, said Consuelo, and she got up and left. So that left R. Louie, me, and Sam, and I wouldn't have left if you'd paid me.

Raising their voices over the sounds of front yard hoots and laffter, Charlie and Violet, so sweet, so sincere, their soft bodies bulging, told a long confusing, rambling story about how they came to social consciousness in late middle-age (somewhere in Missouri or Washington or maybe it was Maine), how they decided to quit their jobs and act on their convictions, they came down the Coast (or maybe it was up the Coast), about how they had finally been directed to Ratouie Louie. (They were sic'd on us, says Consuelo.) Their idea was to organize masses of people to protest the nuclear arms race, who would gather on the lawns of state capitols all across the USA, from Sacramento to Boston, wearing bandages and head dressing spotted with fake blood, and wigs from which they would pull tufts of hair leaving them bald and mottled pates. Instead of shouting slogans and carrying signs, they would break into loud whooping and coughing, heaving and retching, emitting great waves of pretend throw-up. They got radiation sickness, see? Charlie and Violet would walk among the victim-crowds carrying tongue blades and their medical bags.

We tried all afternoon and late into the night to get them to try something else. We were sore from sitting, hoarse from talking, but couldn't get this concerned couple who had about as much savvy as a brass spittoon to change their minds. Don't mourn. Organize, shouted Charlie. That's right, honey, that's right, shouted Violet. We're here to organize. And we've come to ask your help.

So that's what we did. We helped. All of us. We heaved to, pardon the pun, and put on an anti-nuke demonstration the likes of which had never before been seen in this hemisphere. Let's just do it, do it right, and get it over with, said R. Louie. We scattered that week, called in all the markers, some calling in favors, some applying pressure and threats, some making promises they prayed they wouldn't have to keep, all of us doing this and doing that, and no one wanting anyone to know exactly what the other had done. We didn't talk any more than we had to. It could have been our finest hour. We were mighty embarrassed but we did the job. And the thing is, it was a huge success. The press got wind of it right off the bat. They played it up for all it was worth. We all spent a lot of that month hiding out in the storeroom and kitchen of the Drop Anchor Inn while news people poked around Broderick and Bryte trying to get interviews. Charlie and Violet appeared on three different TV talk shows before the demonstration. The Nuke Puke was on everyone's lips. The First National Nuke Puke. You heard it everywhere. You heard it on the streets, in buses, in bars. And it was going to take place right here in Sacto, California.

On the day of the event crowds gathered on the northeast lawn of the Capitol (Over my dead body, the Governor yelled.) People came from the East Bay Area. They came from Sonoma County and Marin County. They came from San Francisco and San Jose. Maybe they came to laff or to scoff but they stayed to play-pretend and protest. They grabbed their stomachs and dropped to their knees. They retched, they heaved, they gagged. Thousands of folks spent almost an hour throwing up at the feet of the legislature, writhing on the lawns and puking near the seat of government, while four gospel choirs sang, "We've Got Radiation Sickness" with lyrics that were written by Bones Maroni, set to the tune of

"The Battle Hymn of the Republic." Two hundred and fifty-seven Cub Scouts and Brownies gathered at the East Entrance to shout, We Want to Live! We Want to Live! while two hundred and twenty-five semi-professional tap dancers shuffled and time-stepped around the Capitol sidewalks chanting, No More Nukes! No More Nukes! As a grand finale, 10,000 pounds of curds and whey were dumped from fast, low flying bi-planes sent up from Sonoma Aerosport. What a day. What a heck of a day. Beautiful, beautiful, sobbed Charlie and Violet. It was beyond our wildest dreams. Thank you. God bless you all.

We're the first to admit maybe things got a little out of hand. But what could we do? The people must be heard. It's the American Way.

Curds and whey ain't the American Way, said a commentator on the nightly TV news. So what does he know? Besides, that wasn't really our idea. That was a little surprise present from one of R. Louie's ILWU buddies from Petaluma. Anyway, fast as we could, we hustled Charlie and Violet onto the first bus out, a bus to Denver. Then we lit out for the Coast.

Last night a pal (who doesn't want to be identified) called and said they'd just about got the curds cleaned out of the palm trees and vacuumed off the State Capitol lawn. So we figure we can leave Bodega Bay about any day now and head back to East Yolo County. Back to home, sweet home. I'm wondering if Charlie and Violet made it to wherever they were going. And what on earth do you suppose they're doing now?

The Beach

Pop named it The Beach so that folks would know that there was actually a beach for the grownups to sit on and the kids to play on. Louie Maroni and his wife Bella renamed themselves Pop and Mom Maroni to give the place a family atmosphere and so that everyone would know who was The Boss. Everything had been built with Maroni family hands. The cabins, the campfire area, the grocery store, the family house.

Pop had wanted to build everything out of round river stones like that auto court he'd seen near Modesto but it didn't work out. Instead all the buildings were built of wood. The cabins were painted white with red doors and red trim. The driveways and turnarounds and flower beds were all outlined with rocks painted marshmallow white. Each cabin had a barbeque pit to the side and a shower attached to the back. The family house also had an outside shower, because, as Mom said, It's awful nice standing under the water under the sky in the sunshine getting clean.

In 1931 Pop and the family built six more cabins on the half acre next to the original court, and that fall and winter he put in a camp and picnic grounds on the one-and-a-half acres that sat next to Beach Cabin Two. There was nothing fancy but there was everything that you'd need, and everything was clean. Neat, clean, and tidy, Mom said. You don't want things fancy when you travel, you want things neat, clean, and tidy. You want to rest on clean bedding on a mattress that don't sag and be ready for the next day. You don't want fancy. You don't need fancy.

Bones and his brothers worked at The Beach during summers and holidays. They were good boys. Both sides of the family visited The Beach every year for rest and reunion, and they pitched in to help too. No one complained. It was fun. Uncle Frankie visited for two weeks every summer and played the piano for dancing on the screened-in side porch that comfortably held six couples. When Bones was nine, Uncle Frankie, the Master of Rags, Honky Tonk, and Slow Struts, taught Bones to sing and play "Don't Jazz Me, Miss Lewellen." That's for me, said Bones. Words and music. Hot damm. That's what I'm gonna be. A words and music man. Good for you, Bones. A balladeer. A troubadour. Smart kid, sang Frankie, striking a chord meant to turn tides.

The camp and picnic grounds were a special joy to Pop. He drove to a wholesale nursery outside of Vacaville to purchase a dozen tiny pines (eight lived) to perpetuate the memory of his and Mom's camping trip to Donner Lake. Their honeymoon actually, where they walked hand in hand along the moonlit dusty roads and played on the beach in the sunshine. They skipped stones on the icy mountain lake and picked gooseberries with a group of fellow campers. They lay in their tent late at night with the flaps up and breathed the piney air and listened to the trees high up murmuring deep in the scented wind. They read to each other from Jack London's *Valley of the Moon*. They promised always to be kind. They had never heard or smelled such wonders and for the rest of their years together they never lost the shine of the memory of that piney-sweet week. That sweet week when they swore lifelong love to each other.

The day they left their granite and pine, sky-blue paradise Pop covered the palms of his hands with pine pitch so they'd have the sharp smell after they went down the Valley to their cannery worker lives. They laughed like a couple of fools when Pop's hands stuck to the steering wheel so bad that Mom had to take over and drive them home. They never visited Donner Lake again but they planned it every summertime. Donner Lake, their Lake of Shiny Dreams. Let's go to the Lake of Shiny Dreams they'd whisper as they lay close and held tight to each other in the Valley's hot dark.

When they got the chance to buy the property on the Sacramento River, with room to build the grocery and cabins, they took it in a minute and never looked back. They would recreate for always that wonderful summer week, and just as good, maybe even better, they'd give other people like themselves a chance at their own week of rest and dreams, their own week of romance.

They're all gone now. Pop, Mom, Uncle Frankie. Bones and his brothers all scattered around the Valley. Even so, today when you drive north along the river road about two miles past Rio Vista you can see real plain what remains of The Beach. Only two structures stand but nothing has been built on the property since. You can walk to the water, sit there on the beach and listen to the lapping sound. No one will bother you, tell you to go away. You can sit down under a pine tree, maybe doze a little. You might hear a screen door slam or hear the sound of couples in love laughing. You might hear someone skipping stones.

Dear JoAnne

The women have no dues to pay.

Dear JoAnne

I'm housesitting again. At Lisa's. Watching the dog and kitty. Why is it when I sit in other people's houses, empty without them, I remember Ross, Ross Grammar School, our grammar school, "those days?" Why is it? I don't know. But I know I'll never forget when I saw *Black Beauty* with Joan McCormick on a Friday night at the Tamalpais Theatre. She went into such paroxysms of sobbing, and Oh no, Oh, my God, I can't stand it, sobsobsob, she really scared me, and although I was deeply embarrassed, I marvelled at the intensity of her emotion over a story we had all read in class and knew the ending. Remember how she and Diane Costigan used to wear the hairs from the tail of Man O' War around their wrists until Miss Patterson made them take them off or else go home? As though those old hairs could do anyone harm, but I guess she was as much at a loss over that as I was there in the theatre with Joan. Only Miss Patterson had some authority.

I once wrote a thing about Miss Patterson, about two pages of stuff. I hope no one ever finds it. I've looked for it several times so I can throw it away, burn it. It's very sentimental, a touch maudlin — Forgive me, Miss Patterson. Not that I don't mean forgive me, Miss Patterson. I mean exactly that. I don't think I've ever been so cruel to anyone in my life. We all were. She must have appeared a victim to us. Even though I was such a little person, I thought her tragic. When I looked at her I felt bad, then flushed with anger, and wanted to punish her for provoking those feelings. What did I sense about her experiences that bothered me so?

Remember how she told us about spring in Montana and the ticks? And how beautiful the state was? That hick tick state, we thought. Oh sure, tall, skinny, pale person, sure, uh huh. She had been principal of a grammar school in Montana, and now she was only vice-principal in Ross. So what did *that* mean? *Demotion* loomed in my mind. What could be more ironclad as a reason for suicide than to be in a state of demotion? Why leave a place she clearly loved and accept a demotion? Well, I never asked, nor did you or anyone else I remember. It was too risky.

I can still smell her face powder, see her watery eyes, hear her odd, controlled voice. And God, JoAnne, I put pins in her afternoon tea! You remember how she liked her tea in the afternoon. One of us poured water in her desk drawer. Another put thumbtacks in her chair cushion. We did this when she was out of the room. We did it quietly. She accepted it quietly. Oh God. We had a collective, a "let's kill Miss Patterson" group. But later we felt contrition and grief, so much so that at Christmas we loaded her down with gifts, inappropriate gestures of the guilty, gaudy and of little value — multi-colored bath beads, new on the market — and the perfect teachers' gifts: writing paper, cologne, and pin-cushions. My parents never allowed me to give a teacher a present, so I bombarded her with cards and hung on her in a smarmy way.

She wore dresses of crepe and dresses of gabardine. Maroons and navy blues, greys and forest greens. She wore her hair in a tight and greying halo fallen to the base of her skull. I can see her now, walking down Shady Lane, looking down, alone and lonely, walking home at the end of the school day to the room she rented down by the San Anselmo line, the ragtag end of Ross, that in itself suspicious, grounds to be wary. Why didn't she live close to the center of Ross, the center where all blessings flow, where everything is clear, defined, where we could relax because we knew where we were, where we were going —nowhere. Oh, the heavenly peace of it, the sweetness of knowing you are going nowhere, for there is nowhere to go. You are already there. There, right in the middle of Ross, California. And there goes poor old Miss Patterson, walking all alone into the outer limits, where the world lies. God, I could weep, JoAnne. And what was her first name? Do you remember? Do you think she really had one? That woman was a prize winner. Just thinking of her makes me feel sad and mean. *Yoohoo, Miss Patterson, hello out there. I'm sorry. I'm so sorry. Hey, it's me. It's Mary Anne, Miss Patterson. Remember me?*

Miss Patterson made me restless. To be raised in Ross made me restless. There we were, plunk in the middle of where everyone else wants to be. But I don't buy that. I don't buy it for a lot of reasons.

But I'll always be in Ross, and I'm still in love with the West where I never got to go because I was already there. Was ever a girl so cruelly gypped? I want to go West! I cried when I was five, standing plumb in the middle of our living room where my Father and his male friends were talking. Go West? my Father said, If you go any further West, you'll drown. And everyone laughed. And there you have it. From that time on, I never recovered. At that radical core, the trouble began. That my Daddy would join in laughter with those bums was a blow from which King Kong could not have recovered. You'll pay for that, Daddy. What betrayal, abuse of friendship, treachery, and all for a cheap, late afternoon laugh.

In Chinatown, with my Chinese uncles, on our way back from the World's Fair on Treasure Island. Look way down, thousands of feet into the bottom of the ravine, down by the tiny thread of a river, down by the red fallen rock, and there you see four Chinese men, one California Poppy Man, and one little girl whose eyes are beginning to cross and no one knows it yet but her, and they won't until she insists that she sees the movies at the Tamalpais Theatre on the walls instead of the screen. Is that a whirlpool I see? What is that at the bottom? Is that Mary Anne in her paper hats that she made one afternoon, the flower petals safety-pinned to the hem of her dress, curling into the vortex, shouting, I want to go West! But no, that's no whirlpool. That's nothing but Ross, California, and they're trying to suck me into it.

Reversing the force of that whirlpool has been my lifetime's work. And also trying to remember the last name of that poor soul Greta, the German girl, daughter of that rough-looking working man who lived in the house that sat on the disputed San Anselmo/Ross Village boundary, so that that unfortunate girl with the hay-colored hair had to go to Ross Grammar School. She arrived in the seventh grade, stayed through the eighth, and graduated in a soft, sad dress. I would like to hear *her* reminiscences of Ross.

I only saw her once after the grammar school graduation. That was when I was about twenty, and we were on the Greyhound bus going to San Francisco. She still lived in that house on the border line. She worked in the City. She looked the same only she wore lipstick and smiled at me, something she never did in school because she hated me. Why I never knew. It hurt my feelings but what could I do? Invite her up to play? Well, hardly. Mother's eyebrows would have shot up and hung on the rafters, and I would have to hear that old saw about how they are just as good as we are, we want you to know that, but they can't reciprocate with invitations and parties like ours, so it is only fair not to encourage these star-crossed associations. All of which translated to: Darling, what is this fascination you have with those people? Tell us, sweetheart. Why do you smile at Negras, talk to chippies, sit with Filipinos, ride beside Jews on the bus? They don't *want* you to ride with them, smile at them. Is it to hurt us? Why, why are you doing this to us? Now give us a smile. No? You can't give us a smile? Well, you are excused to your room. Don't come down until you have a smile on your face. You are so much prettier when you smile. Won't you give your Daddy a smile. We have given you *everything*! they cried.

I don't want *everything*! I cried. Silence. Gasp. Quiet. Suck in air, pinch your nose up a teeny bit. Make your forehead a little stiff, not too much now. Don't make wrinkles. Don't make your face ugly, hear? It'll freeze that way. But definitely go quiet, be stunned, stricken. You could hear a sorority pin fall, a fraternity pin drop — FREEZE! Freeze, please! And there you have the story of life at 77 Wellington Avenue, Ross, California. Frozen into perfection, the postures of perfection. We were Westerners. We were the California Sunshine Poppy family. Oh, what a pretty sight. See the living tableaux. See them at the Meadow Club, see them in church, see them tea dancing, see them at the Santa Barbara Biltmore. See them on the patio shooting one another with little bows and arrows.

JoAnne, remember Madam Boris? My piano teacher? Did you know she wildly protested putting the Japanese in concentration camps in 1942, organized public protests and public drives for clothing and money? She and my Father used to have hissing, spitting fights, bent-over-at-the-waist fights. Now, Benton! Well, she died in the mid-fifties. She's gone, left her beautiful house to her Ross policeman nephew who later became a San Francisco M.D., doctor of the rich. Life is strange, isn't it? Is it anything else?

God, JoAnne, my arm is stiff, stinging, sore. I do not sleep well, but it is not lying down I want. My mouth is dry. I feel energized like protein in a lightning storm. I'm just greatly restless for rest. I want to laugh, Ha Ha, and shout, Hey, Hey, Mother, I didn't hear you. Honestly. Sigh. Mary Anne, you are so theatrical. Mother, I feel funny, I don't know, I just feel very odd. Sigh. Well, then, I guess you feel too odd to go to Santa Monica with us and go shopping in Beverly Hills. Yes, Mother, I guess I do. (Does this mean that people who feel odd are left out of the good times, left out in the cold? Yes, it must mean just that.) No, Mother, I'm sorry. You're right. Here's a little joke, a sweet little smile, a cute little dance step. And even though I don't have dimples, I can make you think I have. A never-pausing cycle of wish-complaint, wish-complaint — the secret of me.

But, there were the wonderful times. I always thought we did far more interesting things than most of the other Ross families. For instance, at the first sign of spring, even when it was so chilly we had to bundle up, we had a big dinner packed so that when Father came home we could all go out to McNears Beach, build a fire, eat by the water, listen to it lapping onto the pebbly shore. And I would wear my rubber bathing shoes so that in any waters I was fearless and protected. No broken glass or rusted tin to tear my feet, no ooze or slime for me. We had our dinner in a grove of eucalyptus trees. Nasturtiums tumbled down the hill and poison oak budded in the undergrowth. Or we would take our dinner out to one of the under-bridge spots around Lagunitas or on the road to Olema. We went swimming in the waterholes and stayed late on school nights because sometimes looking at the stars is more important than getting your sleep, like the night of the meteor shower. One time a friend came along and set up her cello by a buckeye tree in the meadow and played before dinner. She was one of the earliest prisoners of war in China to be released through some kind of diplomatic intervention. She loved China and longed to return. She was remote and lost to us forever. Sometimes we would go out to the San Rafael ferry and take a round trip ride and eat hot dogs the whole way. Always, at the drop of a hat, we would drive to the top of Mt. Tam and pick wildflowers, and my Father would take movies of the deer. Those were lovely days and nights.

Now, it's Monday morning, my last housesitting day. Maybe I'll get a job today or some money or some good news in the mail. God, I just checked on kitty. She peed on Lisa's bed. That's not good. Lisa told me never to let kitty on her bed. It's my fault. I cannot be trusted. I admit it. So, stand me against the fence and shoot me! Go on, I deserve it. Run me down with your car, go ahead. I'll thank you for it. I know I've done wrong. Kick me off the porch, hit me with a dirt clod. But *please*, please don't put pins in my afternoon tea.

So long for now, dear friend. Love from the Old Sock,

Mary Anne

Juke Box Dancer

Is there a place I can go? the old woman wonders. Somewhere I can dance to a juke box? Is there a place where older folks go? Some tavern maybe, a roadhouse, or an unfrequented bar where a juke box stands ready and a silken dance floor lies smooth, waiting for people who value just that: juke box dancing.

When she was little, her parents drove her all over the state, north and south, around the valleys, up into the foothills, along the Delta, out to the beach, stopping at coffee shops and small cafes to eat hamburgers, drink coffee, and dance to the juke box. She thrilled to watch them, so sweet out there on the floor, so silent, just stepping, gliding in harmony, so together, so handsome and rich, dancing and humming along. She thrilled too, when the waitress shouted, Will you all get on in here or your food'll get cold? She loved to watch them where she thought them nicest, where she loved them most.

Later, she and a friend taught dancing in San Rafael. They took their own lessons from ten until three, taught from three to eleven, then raced out with friends to the Yacht Club, the Alibi, the Starlight, anywhere they could dance until two. They loved it. Loved to know they would dance again tomorrow, and the day after tomorrow. Her favorite men were the ones who drove her around, then stopped to dance. In roadhouses, fancy hotels, beer joints, saloons, wherever a juke box glowed with primary colors, or stood etched with orchids, or displayed couples caught in a jitterbug swing. She collected "No Dancing Allowed" signs and stored them in her lingerie drawer. She laughed and felt good. She looked good. To her, juke box dancing resembled an art. She felt special, creative. It smoothed out her restlessness like long ribbons, made it feel almost good.

It's hard to tell it now. It's hard to make people understand what you mean or get them to feel what you felt. When you were a young, good-looking woman, with a closet full of clothes, in a small town in Marin County in the 1950s, you were already in trouble. And when you were a sexy young woman in the fifties with dangerous, advanced ideas, you were close to death. Now, as then, when you can't remember what it was you so passionately wanted and fear there may never be anything you desperately want again, when you can't remember and can't forget, then you keep on taking those long, scented baths, keep on wearing those fine quality clothes, keep on cruising Fourth Street, and keep on feeding those nickels, dimes, and quarters into that big glowing box. You keep on laughing. Keep taking those "No Dancing Allowed" signs down off the walls. You point your toe and touch your stocking. You step out onto that floor. And, Sister, you keep on dancing.

You Could Have Named Her Grande

Nowadays, if you named a girlchild Flossie, right away we'd all think of dental floss. The little boys in her class would tease, and yell, Hi, Dental Floss, Dental Floss, There goes Dental Floss, Come on, let's see your cavities, hahaha.

But in earlier times, what did a mother or father or grandma have in mind when they named the new child Flossie? What does that word mean? Flossie must be short for Floss but what is Floss? Does it mean something clean or shiny, like the word, "gloss?" No more of this nonsense. We'll go right to the dictionary:

floss, *n.* rough silk enveloping silkworm's cocoon; silk, this used in cheap silk goods; candy; floss comes from the word flock.

So now, a whole new light dawns. If you think your daughter will grow up to be something that holds and protects a worm, then name her Flossie. If you believe your daughter will grow up to be someone to be chewed up and swallowed like candy, then please, call her Flossie. If you imagine your daughter will grow up to be cheap silk, by all means call her Flossie. And if you fear your daughter will grow up to be just one of the flock, call her, I insist, Flossie.

But don't expect me to come over on Sundays. And don't you come over here. Don't expect me to hold your hand in a lightning storm. And don't call on me to pick up your meds at the drugstore because, personally, that makes me sick. You could have named her something grand, like Grande. You could have named her Noble.

You could have named her Victory. But you didn't and now it's too late.

So go on, put that cup down, slide that cookie back on the plate, and go on. Who invited you over here anyway? Get on outta here and go name some other girls candy, flock, and worm-house. You've got work to do. Go on. Here's your hat, what's your hurry. Get on outta here. I don't want your company. I may get lonely on somedays but I never get *that* lonely.

So, thanks Ma for naming me Mary Anne. If I had a girl, I'd name her Equality.

The Woman Who Likes to Fall Down

You know how middle-aged and old women are always afraid to fall down? Especially the poor ones? Well, when I lived in Sacramento, I used to see these women who were afraid to step off curbs. They tried to hang onto strangers' arms or they'd clutch at someone's sleeve. They turned kind of sideways, crab-like, to step off a two-and-a-half-inch curb. They stopped the flow of pedestrian traffic while they shot off sparks of fear and stared hard at the ground. When they got off the bus it was even worse. Slower too. Sometimes it was downright painful to watch. They weren't women with any kind of physical defects. They weren't blind or lame or anything like that. These women just plain terrified of falling down. Thank heavens that I was quasi-tolerant. Because that is the way I became a couple of years ago.

I really got scared to fall down when I got to be so poor. First of all, I thought that if I fell down and badly hurt myself, I'd have to be hospitalized, which I couldn't afford, with either a broken wrist or broken arm, even worse, end up with a twisted and sprained ankle. Or, worst of all, break both my ankles. I could almost hear them snap. Later, when I got a piddling little job and was earning some money, I was afraid that I'd step on a pebble that would knock me off balance and I'd fall and break my leg and not be able to go to work. Someone else would get my job. Out in the cold again. Who would help me? Take me in? Who would take care of my dogs?

I was always careful not to walk on the eucalyptus leaves and berries along the side of the road because I remembered how once, when I was little, my bike skidded on those pretty and innocent looking little things. Wherever I walked I picked out the smoothest surfaces available. I tried to keep an even, calm pace. I couldn't afford to get careless and dart around, maybe dash into some pothole hidden in the grass. I ferreted out all the gopher spots around the yard, all the indents in the lawn, all the sneaky, nasty places waiting to snag my toe, pitch me over, end my life as I knew it. I no longer walked in the fields of tall grass.

I wondered if I was getting neurotic. But I remembered that all middle-aged women who were poor felt the same. No, my fears were real. If I fell down then bad things would happen. I would lose the little I had. I would have to start over. I don't mean to imply that my life was governed by fear of this dreaded event. No, not by a long shot. But I was careful. Watchful. I was cautious.

One day I took my dog Violet out to the shed to put her on her yard leash. As we entered the shed her chain caught on a loose board. She yanked her head back, and I lunged forward, landing on the uneven floor. Oh God, no, I thought going down. Oh sweet Jesus. Landing with a thud, I half-sat, half-lay, cold with dread, wondering where I was hurt. But nothing seemed to hurt. Suddenly, I swear to God, I felt a surge of highly charged energy sweep over me. I felt wonderful. Like I'd received some kind of beneficial zap or been shot with a health-giving ray gun. When my body hit that shed floor something vital was released. And I was better for it. In fact, I *liked* it. It felt good!

I wanted it to happen again. I wondered when it would.

Airstream

I have always wanted to live in one of those round-cornered, silver Zepplin cloud-like Airstream trailers. My Uncle Harry had one in 1941. I want to live in an Airstream trailer out in a field, grow flowers and tomatoes in a number ten lard can, wear hats and funny funny clothes. (Look, Ma, Look! That scarecrow! It's moving! Ma! It's moving! — —-SSSHHEEWWW. SShew, Child, and RUN. Go get your Pa. And hurry! Tell him to bring his gun!)

Living in an Airstream trailer is a little or a lot like being on a boat. You can feel your footsteps. You can feel the bounce and sway of the craft on the air-water. I know.

Uncle Harry parked his Airstream on Grandma's lawn in Orangevale that summer out by the huge shed near the mulberry tree, under the oak. I camped out in it. During the night I couldn't go into the house to go to the bathroom because I was convinced that if my feet touched even one blade of grass on the lawn, I'd die. So I'd *hold it* as long as I could. Then I'd open the trailer door, hang onto the door handle, swing out in the door's half-circle, and pee into the night.

GRACEFULLY AFRAID

The blossoms cut through the rain on a diagonal line.

Gracefully Afraid

I have a friend who never does anything right. I don't mean morally. Socially. What I mean is, she won't be respectful when it would benefit her; she won't flirt; she won't color her hair; she won't lose weight. She won't dress herself up; she won't wear makeup. She just won't try to get along. She wears the worst damned looking shoes you ever saw.

They're comfortable, she says.

Well, so what, is what I say. Who wants to be around anyone who wears shoes like that? No man wants to walk down the street with a woman who is fifty-two years old, whose hair is turning grey, who's forty pounds overweight, whose idea of dressing up is a pink sweatshirt, and who wears shoes that look like that.

I personally know of a court case she lost because she refused to call the judge Sir, or Your Honor, during the *entire* proceeding. I was furious. I could have killed her. I went to a lot of trouble during that case. I drove her to the lawyer's office several times. I listened while she ranted and raved about justice and injustice and the class system. I sat with her through the whole mess. And she blew it. On purpose. I know that's why he decided against her. All that work. All that time. All that energy down the drain. She owed it to her lawyer, she owed it to me, and she certainly owed it to herself to sit up there and act right. She wasn't rude, don't get me wrong. She answered all the questions with a complete and intelligent response, but that's not what we're talking about. I tried to call him Sir and Your Honor a couple of times, she says. I couldn't get it out of my mouth, and that's the truth. Huh! The truth. It still burns me up to think about it. It's not as though she stood there and made a heroic political or social statement or anything like that.

If she made even the slightest effort with her looks she would be damned attractive. She is now. Almost. In a certain way. But she won't try. And she says she will never again pay to have her hair cut. She will never again sit still while someone cuts her hair. So she wears it in a long lank down her back or folded up on her head with two giant bobby pins holding it down. It looks like a big cow plop with straw sticking out.

Don't laugh at my hairdo, she says. I don't like that.

Well, I'm not laughing on purpose, just to hurt your feelings, I say. You'd laugh too if you ever looked at it from the back. I don't mean to hurt your feelings, but if something is funny, it's funny.

Okay, she says, but I never laugh at *your* hair.

Well, of course she doesn't. Every hair of mine is in place. I don't set one foot out the door if my hair doesn't look just right. If your hair looks lousy, you look lousy all over. If you look lousy, you feel lousy. The first thing I do after my morning shower is apply my makeup. Before I do my hair, I apply my makeup.

It's a work of art, she says.

I'll show you how to do it, I tell her. I've told her that a thousand times over the years. Never mind, she says, that's okay. During the time I've known her she must have spent a thousand dollars on nice cosmetics, but she just takes them home and puts them in a drawer. What a waste. She doesn't do that anymore. Thank God. I hate to see that kind of waste.

I love your sense of ritual and discipline, she tells me. It's true. I understand things in a certain way and I benefit from that. You see the results of my work. She works, but you don't see the results. She isn't lazy. Far from it. It's just that she doesn't have a tight routine. So she does a little of this and a little of that. But nothing shows. No one room in her house is clean on the same day as any other. She is *not* dirty. No way. I couldn't be friends with someone who is dirty or lazy. But her place is always cluttered. Messy. I admit there's a certain charm to it. It gives the impression that she's hard at work on some emotional or intellectual task. Sometimes there is mystery and excitement around her place. I sit on her couch while she's in another room and feel as though she's going to haul out a canvas she's painted in secret. Or she's going to walk in carrying a manuscript she'll slam down on the table. Some literary masterpiece she's written while I wasn't looking. That's one of the things about her I like: she gives the impression she's somewhere in the wings, doing great, creative work. Or that she's behind the scenes developing a new school of philosophical thought. Of course, that's not the reality. The reality is that she's in her advancing middle age, with no good job, no steady job, with an almost-college degree which is worse than no degree at all because she has no money to go back to school. And besides, by the time she gets back to school, if she ever does, they'll have changed the requirements so she'll have to start all over again, and her past work will have been for nothing. The reality is she's headed for complete disaster. (She doesn't even own an iron. Says she did something with it, but can't remember what!) Sometimes she can't pay the rent; sometimes she can't feed her animals; and sometimes she doesn't have one thin dime in her pocket. I worry about her a lot. But it's her own damned fault.

Don't worry about me, she says, it's not helpful.

I can't help worrying about you.

Then it's *your* problem, not mine.

Well, that's gratitude for you. Thanks a lot, I tell her. Don't call me up the next time you need money for dog food. Don't turn to me when you need a ride job-hunting. Just don't call on me.

Okay, I won't, she says.

Don't, I say.

Now that that's settled, she says, let's talk about something else. Let's talk about you for a change. I know what. Let's go for a drive to Bodega Bay. I'll pay for the gas.

We'll charge it on her gas card, she means. Through the worst of times, she's held onto that. She was homeless once. Literally. Out in the streets, but she had that card. It's my ticket to ride, she says.

We love to go for drives. We see the same sorts of things. Along the Russian River, out to Jenner, up the coast to Fort Ross, or up the Napa Valley. When she had some money, we drove to Vacaville for dinner at the Nut Tree once a week. When we could stand the traffic, we drove to Berkeley to the Claremont Hotel, or to Norman's to eat giant artichokes and walnut pie.

She was a sharp dresser. I felt good walking up the street with her. Not now. She is not one of those women who can throw on rags and look like a million. But one thing that makes me feel good about myself is that, embarrassed or not, I am the kind of person who does not abandon another person because of what she wears or doesn't wear. It's uphill work a lot of the time. Sometimes though, it's fun when we go someplace nice and I'm dressed up and she's not. It's bold and defiant. I feel like people envy my courage and loyalty. Other times, it's not fun at all. It's downright humiliating. I feel she's asking too much of our friendship. More and more I feel that way.

We're getting older and we should try our best. But she says, No, I did that for forty years. That's half my life. She said that right after she dreamed she was going to live to be eighty-one. We tell one another our dreams. We like our dreams. We feel friendly toward them, even when they're a little frightening. It's a bond between us. We're both relaxed about what our unconscious minds might cough up during the night. After she told me that dream, she said, Now, that's it. The next forty years are mine. I said, Good for you! I had no idea she was talking about not wearing skirts anymore, about letting herself go.

She used to have a beautiful body. Now it's hidden under those forty extra pounds. Mine is out there, highly visible. You've got a great body, she says. Well, I ought to, I reply.

I work darned hard to keep it that way. I work out in the gym every day. There's not an ounce of fat on me. I run every day. When she runs, she wets her pants. That's not her fault. I know that. She's had kidney infections since she was young. She could do yoga. But she won't. She even likes yoga. She used to do it with her daughter-in-law. It's getting down on the floor, being out of this world she says she doesn't like. So, she's flabby and I'm not. I'm fifty-one years old and still look great. Like it or not, we get more high marks when we look good in bathing suits.

We both read the same books, and I understand feminist principles. But what is, is. We have to get along in the here and now. This is a man's world and until that changes, we have to do certain things. We have to say certain things; we have to look a certain way. Like it or not. When she kicks up a fuss, I tell her she's just kicking the slats of her cradle.

You know, it's funny. When we first met eighteen years ago, she didn't know beans about being angry or getting revenge or having a good toe-to-toe fight. That's one of the things she liked about me. You don't pretend to any of the virtues, she said. You get even when someone does you dirt, and you don't have fits of remorse about it. I like that about you. You know anger doesn't kill. I know it too, but I still don't know how to use it. You said *that* to *them*? she'd ask, her eyes popping.

Sure I did, I'd say. So what?

I love the way you say, So what.

When we first met, she'd never given anyone the finger. Hardly swore at all. She couldn't get mad without saying, I'm sorry. Once, when she was sick, I gave her my favorite book on anger, how to express it. She read it, and came off the couch like she was shot from guns. She loved it. She loved it that I gave the book to her. You could say I had a big hand in the kind of person she is today. She's a great one to have in your corner when there's a fight.

But as we get older I get nervous about what she'll do next. I say, Please don't make a fuss.

She says, Don't call sticking up for ourselves making a fuss. Besides, even if we make a fuss, what can they do to us? They've done just about all they can. I'll never be a history professor and you'll never be a Hollywood screen writer. We're just pokey people now, getting old in our pokey places. For God's sake, let's not go to our graves without at least shooting our mouths off, she shouts.

And let's not go to our graves, I shout back, without you looking pretty for at least one day. I can hardly bear to look at you anymore.

She hung up. Who can blame her? I shouldn't have said that. It was mean. If I feel that way about her I shouldn't pal around with her any longer. It's not fair. It's not just a whim, the way she is. Not some stage she's going through. She's not going to change back. I see that. I'd drop her tomorrow. I think about it all the time. But she's fun to be with, like something funny or special or exciting is about to happen. Sometimes people envy me because she's my friend, not theirs. She's attractive in some elusive way. But it makes me furious.

We didn't talk for over three months after she hung up on me. I missed her. But it was a relief not to see her. Not to deal with her anger and insights. Just do my daily routine: relax, read novels, drift, and window-shop. Sightsee and be seen. Pick the daisies and smell the roses, as the old saying goes. But then I thought, Dammit, I want to see her, want to talk to her because there's something I have to say. So, I called her. We got together, had a good time. But things were never the same again. We discovered we were content not seeing each other for long periods. What a relief.

What we differ about most is what's most important: our dignity. The important thing is respect. How do you get respect when you have that gut hanging down over your belt, wear those damned lace-up shoes and your hair's a mess. You obviously don't respect yourself. So, how do you expect anyone to respect you? I ask.

And how can you consider yourself dignified with cleavage like that? she says. How can you respect yourself when you dose you head with dangerous chemicals every six weeks. You're over fifty years old, for God's sake, and you bat your eyes like some silly fifteen-year-old. You spend half your life in front of the mirror. That's not my idea of dignity.

Maybe I do, I say, but I get the good jobs, don't I? I'm not the one who can't pay the rent. I'm not the one who's sick with money worries half her life. The *last* half of her life. Let's be clear about that. You don't even smile at anyone anymore. You still have to live in this world, you know. So what kind of respect are you getting for your trouble? Maybe every two years someone writes from Florida or Washington or God knows where and says he or she likes the story you wrote, but that's only one story. The *only* story you ever published. I hate to throw that up to you because I think you're a wonderful writer. You know I do. But you aren't going to get published anymore. You haven't published a story in five years. And you are never going to get your degree, and we both know that, because you have a crummy attitude. So, where is all this respect you work so hard to get? Go on, show me. Correct me if I'm wrong, but I don't see any lying around here. There isn't any manifested in your refrigerator. You don't even have margarine, for crying out loud. Sometimes you just have to kiss ass, for God's sake. You know that. Tap into reality for just ten lousy seconds!

I don't mean that. We end up yelling. It bothers me. She's very political, very realistic. I say it because I'm mad at her, and I worry about her. It's like having a friend who has a disease that medication can help. When the friend won't take the medication, you get mad. It's like that. The disease we both have is being born women in a man's world. It's not a nice disease and it's a progressive disease. But you don't have to die from it. It doesn't have to be fatal. That's scary.

Well, I've just about had it. I love her and I know she loves me. I love all the fun we've had over the years, and I love the times we've helped each other out of jams and through bad times. But I *don't* want to write protest letters to wardens of women's prisons. I want to write shopping lists. Expensive shopping lists. I want a nice house and pool to sit by, reading or daydreaming, maybe in St. Helena. I've wanted that for all the years I can remember. I want a husband who is financially secure and generous, who is affectionate. One who won't invade my space. In return for that, I'll give him good meals, good sex, and clean, pressed clothes. That's not such a terrible contract, is it? It would be comfortable and peaceful. But I could never trust her in that kind of environment. Not that she'd be rude. But she couldn't be trusted. Something bad would happen.

It shames her and makes her mad, she says, the way I hang around the golf course, the tennis courts. But I play golf, dammit, and I play tennis, and that's where I'm going to find a St. Helena man. Just because I haven't found one during the past twenty years proves nothing, no matter what she says. It only proves I haven't found him yet; not that I won't. And when I do find him, she won't be an asset. I take that back. Men like her. She makes them laugh so she'll seem an asset until they get to know her. After that, they'll think she's a Communist. I'll be tarred with the same brush, and I'll kiss that house and pool goodbye. Please don't recoil as though I'm some kind of monster, because I'm not. I'm a woman who will be in her sixties in just ten short years. A woman with practically no value anywhere in this world, so I don't intend to be in this world. I intend to be in the small world of the Napa Valley. I intend to grow old gracefully. You can't grow old gracefully if you've spent the last half of your life swimming against the current the way she has. I want to grow old surrounded by pretty things. And I can't do that if I'm worn out with worry because I have a friend who lands in a fleabag flophouse, who lives in poverty, who might get hauled off to prison for associating with terrorists, who could die in a ditch because she has no home. I can't look forward to that. I won't. Sometimes now, when she's talking, my attention fades and I look at her and think: you're going to blow my old age, you old bat. And I hate that.

Last week we went to a powwow at the American Indian University near Davis. I felt lucky to have a friend who was invited to a powwow. I'm glad I went with her. Not that I had a good time. I didn't, but it was an experience that goes into my brain bank. And that enriches me. Next week, I'm taking her to Sebastopol to interview an old woman who was the first female member of the ILWU in Petaluma. That will be interesting. I'm looking forward to it. But it's scary too because I think this old woman's a Communist. Don't worry about it, she says, everyone was a Communist in those days. But I do. What if it comes out ten years from now that I spent the afternoon in the home of a Communist? What then? That would put me into the worst kind of light when I could least afford it. I don't intend to grow old with that kind of fear.

I don't intend to grow old, living on the brink of disaster, frantic and anxious, the way she is most of the time. Don't kid yourself.

I'm a thin-ice skater, she laughs.

That's not funny, I say. That's not something to be proud of.

I don't want to be called from poolside one nice day to bail her out of some two-bit Central Valley jail. I don't want to explain to my future husband that he has to attend the Beaulieu Vineyard Concert-under-the-Stars alone because I have to drive down to Oakland to attend to a batty old woman who was found raped and beaten in a downtown alley, and who managed to whisper my name and phone number before lapsing into a life-threatening coma. I just won't do it.

So, I've made up my mind. After our get-together next week, I'm going to slip over to her place early in the morning. Before dawn. Leave all the books I've borrowed on her front porch.

I don't want to do it that way. But I have to. She'll know what it means. I'm going to miss her like crazy. She'll miss me, too. That's too bad — too bad to end it that way.

But my mind's made up. It comes under the heading: Old Age Security.

The Tiger Lily

Most people weren't quite real to Faye. This characteristic was nearly unconscious on her part, and few seemed to notice. The people in Faye's life were stationed to play out their roles, take their positions, carry the props, or wash the brushes for the great work of art Faye considered her life. Her house was a work of art. Her garden was a work of art. Her clothes and her husband's were works of art. Even her cats and dogs were works of art. Everything. Everything was placed to frame and illuminate the giant canvas Faye labored over so proudly and tenderly all her waking life.

Her nights were filled with anxious sleep, dreams of pain, grief, and torture. She emitted unearthly groans, cries and broken sentences in an unidentifiable voice until someone tiptoed gently in to wake her.

In response to her deep, deep fears of growing old, Faye died at age 65, in a silken gown after dancing all night aboard a cruise ship off the coast of Barbados. Shortly after, a note she had written was found under the kitchen phone. It read: my cupboards are bare.

Epilogue

Red Stone, Blue Stone

Have you ever seen a one-legged man riding a bicycle? I'm not trying to make a joke nor am I leading up to any pointed profundity. I'm simply asking you: Have you ever seen a one-legged man riding a bicycle?

Well, I have. A couple of years ago in Broderick, California, in the parking lot of the Wells Fargo Bank. I looked up from the book I was reading, at the exact moment, in that strange way that we do when our hidden antenna tells us that something is present, something we ought to notice. And there was a man wearing dirty blue jeans and a faded red sweatshirt, coming along beside me on his bicycle. He had only one leg, and he peddled with it. His crutches were tied to the legless side of the bike. He didn't ride in a straight line. Instead, he weaved from side to side, not like someone staggering, but in a purposeful way, as though he found that the best and safest way to ride. His sweatshirt was hooded and he rode with his head down, so I never saw his face. What I saw was a lone-legged, faceless man riding a bicycle under the weak winter sun in Broderick, California, just one-half mile from the muddy Sacramento River. Will you just look at that? I thought. That makes me a monkey's uncle. I wrote the day, the time, and the place in the margin of my book.

I don't know how I could ever include that in a story or slyly insert it into a conversation, so I am writing it down now. Because there are some things that ought to be noted. Some things that must stand alone, unsupported, even though we don't know how they will or why we think they ought to.

Like the time that I was crossing the street in Sacramento and spotted a hunk of aquamarine glass lying in the crosswalk. I almost got run over and killed when I stopped, bent down, and picked it up. But I had no choice. Seldom one finds such a hunk of aquamarine glass, and spots it in such an unexpected place. It sits on the shelf over my sink. When I look at it and pick it up, I see it again as waterblue glass on black asphalt. It makes me smile and shake my head.

Telling that brings to mind the time back in the late '50s when I was taking a sweet, solitary stroll in the countryside outside of Twain Harte in Calaveras County. I had walked about a mile when I decided to climb up onto an old pine tree stump to rest my eyes for a while. When I opened my eyes, I spotted a beautiful piece of smooth, deep red rock lying in the road. It reminded me of the bloodstone ring that, as a child, I had dropped down the floor heater at my mean Grandmother's house in Roseville. I was afraid to tell anyone what had happened because it was the second time in two years that I had lost a ring down that floor heater.

The first ring was an aquamarine ring given me for my birthday. The bloodstone was also a birthday ring. And do you know, no one ever asked, What happened to your birthday rings? At first, I was afraid to hear that question. Later, I was sorry I never did. The year before my father died, I looked at his face on the hospital pillow, and wondered, Aren't you *ever* going to ask me about my birthday rings? I didn't say it out loud. Too bad because my father, in his dark-humored way, would have thought the ring-heater story very funny.

The rock on the road in the mountains looked to me just like the stone from my ring, only larger, more adult.

It was a dense blood red. A rock that must have called out to me. I jumped down from the stump, but instead of picking up the stone, I decided I would kick it home by the back road. What ought to have been a two mile walk turned into four and took at least two hours because I had to zig and zag, stop and start, go front and back, kick and miss, kick again, and sometimes walk in circles to get that stone back without my hands touching it, which was a major part of the plan. When I finally got the two of us into town, my feeling of triumph turned to sorrow and guilt, realizing that I had dislodged and displaced forever the red stone that had probably only called my name in order to say, Hello there. Great day, isn't it? I thought about picking it up and flinging it into the woods behind the house. But, no, let it lay. You've done enough to it for one day. So I bent down and whispered, I'm sorry about this. I feel real bad. I know it doesn't help. And I ran into the house.

The rock was gone when I came out to the road the next day. Maybe a car tire hit it and spun it off into the woods, or maybe it got shattered against a bigger rock. Maybe it grew legs (like our parents told us lost things did) and went home on its own. I don't know. But I never forgot that rock and what I did to it. Furthermore, I always felt too foolish to tell the tale. Embarrassed for myself as though I told the world I would eat only rose petals and call myself Rainbow.

Years ago, in Vineburg, I was having a particularly hard time accepting the fact, which I was warned I must, that I had a chronic, incurable disease. Mostly I had decided it was some kind of trick. A not very nice joke that had gotten out of hand and turned cruel. It was hard to get through those days when I felt so bad and looked so bad that my friends would lower their eyes and turn away.

    I set up a bed in each room of the house except the kitchen and bathroom, which gave me four places to lie down so that I did not feel stuck in one room, and would not feel so much like an invalid. Invalids don't usually go from room to room, I thought. I also set up a bed on the patio so that when I was feeling especially sick and lowdown, I could drag my skeleton-body out into the world like an ordinary person.

    On this particular day I had gone out to the patio. It was fall, my favorite time of the year. I lay in the sun in my yellow robe, admiring the day and loving that robe because of its color, like lemons, its softness against my skin. I rubbed my robed arm across my face and recalled the softness of the hair on a baby's head, the warmth of a hand held in love.

    Eyes closed, I dozed for a long, long time until a sudden darkness fell across my face. It brightened and darkened again. First I thought clouds must be passing in front of the sun. Then I became uneasy as I realized it was too regular for the passing of clouds. Opening my eyes I saw an enormous hawk, long wings spread, circling slowly, slowly, lower and lower, circling the air above my bed. He must have thought he'd found a giant dead baby chick, just feathers and bones spread out over a tiny morsel of meat. Just enough perhaps for a noontime snack. Holy God! I yelled, and jumped up, running back into the house, moving faster than I had moved in over a year. I lay on the floor weak from exertion, weak from dizziness, weak from fright. And weak from laughter. What a wonderful laugh I had that day. Rolling around on the floor, holding my sides. Well, I thought, maybe I am sick after all. That hawk must have thought I was dead. It was a turning point in my life.

One time I found an old, old stick pin handmade out of brass. It was quite large, maybe four inches long. Attached to it was a brass clown with head, arms, feet, and legs that actually moved. Its face and little shoes were made of copper. I found it in a junk shop, among some ratty, dingy scarves that smelled like five-and-dime cologne. It must have been overlooked when the scarf was thrown out to be picked up and sold again. Strange, I thought, that something so big and so bright, so heavy in the hand could be overlooked. But how else explain this very special object lying loose and forgotten in a dusty bin in a cement-floored junk shop on the west end of Fourth Street in Santa Rosa, California? When I took it to the counter to ask the price, the woman-clerk barely glanced at it, as though it were some burnt out match I held in my hand and not a metal work of art. Oh, I don't know, she said, a quarter. A quarter? Only a quarter?

I carried that clown pin around with me for many years in different pockets of this garment or that. I could make it wave its arms. I could make it kick up its legs in a dance. But I could never use it as a stick pin because the tip end was blunt and bent. It wouldn't stick into anything. But I could hold it in my hand, look at the smile on its face and feel myself smile. Just imagine. Only charging me a quarter.

Now this is not a story. These things don't make a story. What I have done is to recall them, bring them forth and relate them in a way that makes them not a story but a relation. These are my relations. I tell them because some things ought to be told. Whichever way they can. These are amazing things. We all have them inside us: things like the one-legged man riding a bicycle. Red and aquamarine stones. Lost rings in fiery furnaces. Circling hawks. Signs and symbols and things we can hold in the palms of our hands. They mustn't be hidden in the heart to be burned with the corpse. Tiny bits of mirrors or colored glass, twisted, weathered wood from days we felt lowdown or days we felt not bad. Scraps of rusty metal and sandwhite shells. We hold them once in our hands and we remember them all of our lives.

Mary Anne Ashley

Mary Anne Ashley lives in Northern California and works at a nearby state hospital. She studied poetry with Kate Rennie Archer at the Dominican Upper School in San Rafael. Her work has appeared in newspapers, in *Quindaro 14* and *Quindaro 15*, in *Midwest Villages & Voices*, and in the Papier-Mache Press anthology on women and aging: *When I Am an Old Woman I Shall Wear Purple*. Her work has also been read on public radio. She is a member of St. Joan's International Alliance, International Workers of the World, and the International Geranium Society. She is working on a new collection of stories about Marin County, California.

Other Papier-Mache Press Books:

When I Am an Old Woman I Shall Wear Purple, an anthology of poetry, fiction, and photography exploring the issues of aging women, $10.00, 0-918949-02-5. "Sheer delight." *Minnesota Women's Press*

Another Language, poetic exploration of aging by septuagenarian Sue Saniel Elkind, photographs by Lori Burkhalter-Lackey, $8.00, 0-918949-05-X. "A grand offering to the dignity of aging." *Pittsburgh Press*

The Tie That Binds, Fathers & Daughters/Mothers & Sons, an anthology of poetry, fiction, and photographs about relationships between parents and children of the opposite sex, $10.00, 0-918949-04-1. "A beautifully produced volume." *Writer's Digest*

The Inland Sea, Poetry by Jenny Joseph, a selection from the poetry of the British author of "Warning—When I Am an Old Woman I Shall Wear Purple," $5.00, 0-918949-08-4. "She can delineate surfaces like a sculptor—exact, precise, sharply definite yet with a startling undertow." *Eastern Daily Press*

Flight of the Wild Goose, Poetry by Janet Carncross Chandler, photographs by Lori Burkhalter-Lackey, an exploration of late-life romance and relationships, $8.00, 0-918949-07-6. "A celebration of age, of the fullness of a life not merely undiminished but genuinely flourishing." Mark Doty

If I Had a Hammer, Women's Work in Poetry and Fiction, an anthology of poems, fiction, and photographs exploring women's experience in the workplace, $11.00, 0-918949-09-2.